DEEP IN THE MIST

A fictional memoir of New Petrograd

HEATHER J. GRAHAM   **DIANA VAN GEFFEN**
LORETTA SCUTCHINGS

Art by Graham Harris

Assisted publication by Moonshell Books, Inc.

Print ISBN 9781677446650

Deep in the Mist / Heather J. Graham et al — 1st ed.

❀ Created with Vellum

INTRODUCTION

In this sequel to *Lighthouse in the Mist*, an old mystery is discovered in New Petrograd's past.

Gaspar, Tony and Daria's son, has moved home to take over Tony's renovation business. He and some of his friends take on a project that will benefit everyone in their village. His old roommates from Calgary, Kevin and Greg, have come to help out. But when a horrifying discovery throws a shadow on New Petrograd's past, the village is in upheaval. Everyone must decide just how far they will go to solve it.

As an officer on the Vancouver police force, June and Marvin's daughter Shelley is the logical person to come to their aid. She works as a liaison among the locals, Constable Freedmont of the Prince Rupert RCMP, and the district coroner's office. These authorities work for some months to untangle this very cold case. But as Shelley becomes more ingrained in village life, people begin to wonder ... Will she leave when the case is concluded? And is she sincerely working on the case, or has she become distracted by romance?

IN THIS SERIES

ACKNOWLEDGMENTS

This book was written by three residents of Carewest Garrison Green long-term care facility, in Calgary, Alberta, Canada.

The authors would like to show appreciation to the following individuals. Doug Martin; Vern Falat; and Scott Darling, President, Performance Energy and Production Services, for their project advice. Anna Borosh for help with everything Russian. Miles Partington from the Calgary Chief Medical Examiner's office. Corporal Mike Klassen, RCMP, for help with the crime scene. Carol-Lyne Carter for providing support with draft edits. Graham Harris for creating the fabulous cover image. Moonshell Books who was so instrumental in helping with the publishing.

We had loads of fun writing *Deep in the Mist* and we hope you have just as much pleasure reading it.

PRAISE

How exciting to be back with old friends (and some new) in the well-loved community of New Petrograd! In the wonderful sequel to *Lighthouse in the Mist*, our authors offer an enthralling mystery and an enchanting romance. I loved reading and learning more about the journeys of familiar characters, as well as meeting some vibrant newcomers. Cozy up with a cup of tea and settle in for a wonderful journey that leads you *Deep in the Mist*. You will not regret it!

— JACQUELINE SWINDELLS

I was born in Russia (Soviet Union) in 1957 and came to Canada in 1981. I had a poor upbringing where often I had difficulty to nourish my body well, but those amazing Russian recipes that are in the book were priceless food that we grew up on and now are able to share with the rest of the world. I loved every page of the book. Each character and each celebration of the daily lives of the heroes deeply touched my heart. If it takes a village to raise a child, I can truly say that you ladies became a village that have raised this book as your special child and I congratulate you on a job well done!

— ANNA BOROSH

I found this sequel to be a great read. I enjoyed spending more time with the characters I met in the first book, but enjoyed being introduced to some more of New Petrograd's residents. I especially enjoyed reading of Gaspar moving home and taking over his papa's renovation business. Along with his friends, they soon found themselves involved in a situation which was more than Gaspar had bargained for and yes, even a new romance appears to be unfolding. I particularly love the recipes at the end of the book. You can make something and then sit down, grab your book, and immerse yourself as if you are sitting at the Borscht Kettle enjoying a meal with some of the locals. Well done to the authors on their second book. I eagerly anticipate the book coming next year, *Changes in the Mist*.

— LORNA HAYES

Deep in the Mist was filled with suspenseful relationships (connections). I wanted to learn about the Russian culture: the people, the food, the parties. The authors provided all of that and more! I found myself getting lost in in the mysteries unfolding in New Petrograd. The introduction of new characters and evolution of those we met in the previous book left me thrilled to read more. Their analysis of the Russian traditions and rituals continues to intrigue and excite!

— FORMOSA CHANCELVIE

Deep in the Mist is a wonderful sequel to the previous book, *Lighthouse in the Mist*, written by Heather Graham, Loretta Scutchings, and Diana Van Geffen. I enjoyed the development of the characters from the first book and the addition of new people who add to the story. I really got caught up in the action and romance that developed. Congratulations on a great read, ladies.

— CAROL-LYNE CARTER

FOREWORD

Deep in the Mist is a second success for Heather Graham, Loretta Scutchings, and Diana Van Geffen as a sequel to their previous book, *Lighthouse in the Mist*. This novel is full of suspense and is a must read as a horrifying discovery throws a shadow on New Petrograd's past. You will be in suspense while all decide how far they will go to solve the mystery. The clear description of people, places, and romance will intrigue one to want to read on. Watch for the results of a satisfying ending of new acquaintances, which often turn into more. I am impressed once again with the selection of great recipes to fit the story, and with the bonus of a glossary for better understanding of terms and wording throughout the book.

— MARGARET BRAUSSE, MANAGER OF
SUPPORT SERVICES, GARRISON
GREEN/ROYAL PARK

PART ONE

Deep in the Mist

CHAPTER ONE

Gaspar Comes Home

Standing on the deck of Joe's barge, Gaspar watched as the crew loaded supplies for the various hamlets that populated British Columbia's Pacific Northwest coast. He eagerly waited in anticipation of their departure. He could hardly believe that only yesterday he had walked out of his apartment in Calgary, flown to Vancouver, and was now part of the cargo on Joe's barge. His destination was the village he had grown up in, New Petrograd. Joe had informed him it would probably take six days of traveling to get there and he could hardly wait for the next six days to be over. Joe had added, "That is, if we have favourable weather."

Staring into the murky waters of Burrard Inlet, where the barge was anchored, a pain ran through his heart whenever he thought of Barbara. At their final parting last week, she had refused his proposal. He could still see her looking at him with clear blue eyes and saying "No." Then she had bent her head of curly red hair, muttering that she really did love him but just did not imagine herself living in a tiny village.

Love me, he thought as he spat into the sea. Not my idea of love.

Was moving home sealing his fate as a bachelor? How was he ever going to meet someone now? Not liking where his thoughts were taking him, he abruptly turned away from the railing and wandered off to seek Joe out.

He found him just coming out of the cabin and when Joe saw him, he smiled and shouted, "Another half hour and we should be steering out to Georgia Strait." As an after-thought, he added, "It seems like just yesterday that you and the Filipov twins were part of my cargo going to Vancouver. The three of you chatted all the way there about how exciting it would be to live in a big city."

"Well, Joe, I've been working in Calgary for five years as a journeyman in a big construction company. I feel my education is complete. I can take over my *papa*'s business doing renovations and maybe even expand on it. It sure feels good to be going home. I've learned that in the end big city life doesn't hold any charm for me. On the prairies I've been so lonesome for the salty spray of the ocean."

Gaspar felt the tremor of the engines as they rumbled to life and the barge started moving. Soon afterwards they cleared the Second Narrows Bridge. As they went gliding along, Joe pointed out the big Ferris wheel at the Pacific National Exhibition. Nothing else in Vancouver was distinguishable, other than perhaps Stanley Park and the Lion's Gate Bridge. Soon they had sailed under the bridge and the barge turned north. With the turn came a flash of excitement... they were on their way!

Once they maneuvered into open water, Joe called Gaspar over and introduced him to his four crew members. Bill was short and stocky. Ray was tall and lean. As for Scott and Brian, their size and shape were indistinguishable. So, Gaspar used other features to identify them. Brian had dirty blonde hair, and Scott had a shaggy head of brown hair and a scar on his chin. Joe informed Gaspar that his crew took turns preparing meals and other housekeeping duties while at sea.

Gaspar quickly offered to help also. "Joe, make use of me any way you think you can." This would make the journey go faster.

Once supper was over, Gaspar retired early that first night. By himself again, his melancholy mood returned. Since Joe's comment about the Filipov twins, Marianne and Mary Ellen, his mind seemed to go racing back to his school days and the girls. Marianne really hadn't been timid in her teen years regarding her crush on him. Those wretched guys, his closest buddies, Brad Rosnokov and Martin Shatrov, made his life miserable with their incessant teasing. Marianne's friend Anna Petrov was even worse, trying every way she could to entrap them. He wondered where Marianne was, and what was happening in her life now. Her plan had been to attend the University of BC to become a teacher. She'd probably earned her degree and was teaching now. Mary Ellen was considering business, probably something like an MBA.

I wonder if they ever go home. As he drifted off to sleep, he was thinking it would be rather nice to see them both again.

As everyone sat on the deck on the third day at sea, Gaspar asked Joe a question.

"Joe, this is something that has been on my mind. I sold my car in Calgary because it really wouldn't be suitable on the bush roads around New Petrograd. I know I can use my *papa*'s old Bronco, but I'm pretty keen on a 1980 Ford F-250. I think for my uses a 250 cubic V8 engine would be adequate."

"Go for a 400 cubic V8," Brian said. "That is what I've been looking at myself."

Gaspar chuckled, while explaining to him there would be no need for the bigger truck in New Petrograd. "In town there are a few rain-rutted streets and the town is surrounded by a few miles of bush roads that don't go any distance to speak of."

Ray also added another thought. "I've been considering a Toyota Land Cruiser. When I read the specs on it, I was impressed, it seems like a great vehicle. You might want to consider comparing them."

Gaspar acknowledged their comments with a nod. He asked Joe, "If I purchased a truck, could you load it on to the barge and bring it to me?"

Joe quickly assured him, "Yes. A few years ago, the barge was rigged with a ramp for loading larger items." Then he asked, "How do you think your dad got his Bronco?"

"I have to admit I hadn't thought of that," Gaspar replied.

Scott added, "If you need someone to help purchase it, I'm your man. I like going auto shopping and it only gets sweeter when someone else is footing the bill."

"Thanks Scott, that would be a great help. I might take you up on that."

The conversation quickly moved on to other things—the Canucks win over the Edmonton Oilers the night before, which they had listened to on the radio; the rising cost of living in Vancouver and the lovely fall weather. Gaspar realized this latter topic was especially important to them because the nice weather certainly made their work more pleasant. He had to admit that the rainy fall and winter weren't something he looked forward to, either. He had enjoyed the clear blue skies of Alberta, even on the coldest days.

When a lull came in the conversation, Scott pulled out a deck of cards. "Who's up for a game of Gin Rummy?"

Joe's four crew members quickly hustled around a table and Scott started dealing.

"Gaspar," Joe said. "I'll take you up on your offer to help me make supper." Then, turning back to his crew, he said, "After supper Gaspar and I will take on the winning team. And the losers, well, you can do the dishes."

Four heads lifted from staring at their hands long enough to acknowledge Joe's comment. "Sure thing, boss."

Then they were intently looking at their hands again as Brian laid down his first card and looked expectantly at his partner. Joe and Gaspar headed to the galley. Gaspar suddenly realized that he was enjoying the camaraderie of the trip much more than he would have imagined. He had enjoyed talking about the Canucks versus the Oilers. Thinking about the Canucks conjured up evenings when Mr. Filipov would invite him and his buddies and their fathers to the lighthouse to listen to a game.

Often, Gaspar stood by the railings just breathing in that indescribable smell of the ocean, which he loved and remembered so well. Each day they stopped at a couple of hamlets. He enjoyed observing the village folk's pleasure as the barge anchored at each place. As kids, they'd been so excited when Joe's barge was spotted on the horizon before docking at New Petrograd. When the barge was moored, he could hear the gentle slapping of the waves against its sides and knew how calm the sea was.

On the sixth day he was standing on the deck, his anticipation ever increasing. Then they turned another corner, and, in the distance, he could see it—the craggy point he knew so well. He was home.

The time after the barge cut its engines and coasted to the dock felt very long. As it drew nearer, Gaspar could see his *roditeli* holding their arms high, waving blue scarves. He lifted his own arm high in an answering wave.

Once the barge docked, it was only a few gigantic steps and Gaspar found himself engulfed in his *mama's* arms. Or should it be said, enfolded in the embrace of his *roditeli* as he felt his *papa* come up behind him.

His *mama*, with an enormous grin, hugged him while saying, "Welcome home, my baby."

"I missed you, my boy. I've have been counting the days until you came home and not only because my retirement is in view," his *Papa* said, as he grinned and gave him a slap on his back.

"I've missed you both, too," Gaspar said warmly, smiling at them as they began to move across the dock, their arms entwined.

Progress was slow, because several people came up to greet him. There was Frank and Betty Yusporov, the owners of the New Petrograd General Store. A few more steps and he saw Martin Shatrov, who happily introduced him to his wife, Gayle, and their daughter, Angela, who was toddling along between her parents.

Bob Petrov gave him a hug. "Come by for a meal." Bob and Olga were the owners of the Borscht Kettle, which served as the village's restaurant and bar. However, he knew Olga best as his schoolteacher. As she came alongside her husband, he bent to embrace her, smiling inwardly as he did so. She really didn't seem scary at all now.

Another stop was made to say hello to Uri Golubov, "Welcome home, old chum." Then in the next breath he said,

"Don't worry about Gaspar's luggage. I'll bring it by later. I'll just borrow my father-in-law's truck."

"Thank you, Uri. I was so excited to see my son I didn't even think of his luggage. We probably just left it sitting back there on the dock."

His *papa* was just concluding his conversation with Uri when Gaspar felt another thump on his back. Turning, he found himself facing John Molodtsov. A little behind John he could see his wife Katarina and Anna Golubova heading their way also. Anna looked to be waddling as she walked towards them and he realized she was very pregnant. He couldn't help but wonder when their baby was due but thought he'd ask his *mama* later.

Alex and Anna Yusporov raced past calling greetings, saying, "We need to get together soon."

As they approached the end of the dock, he saw Phil Filipov and Marg Rosnokova standing together. Marg was leaning into Phil, intently listening to something he was saying, a smile slowly forming on her lips. Then he saw with a start that they were holding hands.

He waved to them, before turning to his *mama*, "Mr. Filipov and Brad and Don's *mama*?"

"Yes," she happily replied while giving him a quizzical look. "Don't you remember me writing you about their romance last summer?"

In response, Gaspar gave his *mama* a shrug.

As they started up Marine Street, walking towards their house, she proceeded to tell him more about their romance.

"From all appearances it looks to be going very well."

As they approached their home, his *mama* pointed at the Pagodon house across the street, noting that a couple from Vancouver had bought it and moved in to retire. She bubbled away as she told him their names were Marvin and June Palmer and how they had learned by accident that June was related to Tatyana Pagodona. She added, "That's a story for June to tell you sometime."

After catching her breath, she continued, "*Papa* and I have enjoyed getting to know them over the summer. Of course, now we are looking forward to spending winter evenings together, visiting or playing games. It's nice having neighbours across the street again, especially ones our own age."

By now Gaspar was thinking how much had changed in the time he had been away from this quiet village, where he had always felt nothing ever happened. He couldn't wait to get together with his old buddies, the few who might still be around. He'd see what other changes they could tell him about. He was also eager to ask Martin in private where he had met Gayle, wryly thinking to himself that Martin had better luck finding a wife than he'd had with Barbara.

When they arrived home, his *papa* said, with a wink to him, "Daria, is it time to delve into the baking you've been preparing for Gaspar's homecoming?"

Starting to dig in the fridge, his *mama's* muffled words came back to them. "My dear, I've seen you sneak a few goodies when you thought I wasn't looking, but overall, I admit, you have patiently waited until Gaspar came home. I wouldn't think of making you wait any longer. I took a *sharlotka* cake out of the freezer before we left for the dock."

Gaspar and his papa looked at each other with a grin. Yes, he thought, it's good to be home.

CHAPTER TWO

Gaspar's Holiday Ends

A week after Gaspar came home, Daria walked into the kitchen one morning to see Tony sitting at the table, absently stirring his coffee and looking at last week's newspaper.

"Good morning," she yawned, going over to give him a hug and kiss.

Returning her kiss, he said, "Good morning to you too. What a lovely maroon sweater you are wearing, my dear."

"Just like yours, except yours doesn't have this beautiful embroidery down the front of it." Then laughing, she added, "Our son has been home for a whole week and he just presented these gifts to us last night. I guess he has finally had some time to start unpacking."

Tony looked over his paper and commented, "He sure has been enjoying getting together with his old buddies. However, I think today I'm going to put a wrench in his fun. I am just about finished the flooring at the Palmers'. They also asked me to do some painting. I think this is a good job to have Gaspar start helping me. We can get twice as much done if we're both working on it. Today I am planning to introduce him to the

Palmers and while we are there, ask Marvin to show us which rooms they want painted."

"Oh," Daria responded as she carried a cup of tea and a plateful of *oladi* and sat down across from Tony. "That will sure please June. She doesn't say anything to me, but I can see the look on her face that she's quite weary with how long the flooring project has taken."

While spreading jam on her *oladi*, she glanced at the empty setting in front of Tony. "Did you have breakfast? Earlier this morning I came down and fried some eggs and made *oladi*."

Tony smiled at her, "I sure did. Thanks for making my favorite, I do like those little pancakes. I have already washed my plate and put it in the cupboard."

"You are a sweetheart."

Tony blew her a kiss before saying, "I really can't blame June. These renovations have taken much longer than they should have."

"Why is that, *Papa*?" Gaspar asked as he came into the kitchen and pulled a chair up to the table.

"Last summer two young chaps, Mark and Steve, sailed in one day and asked Bob Petrov if he knew of anyone wanting renovations done. Marvin and June had just moved to New Petrograd and they were eating supper there that evening. They quickly started a conversation with the guys and ended up hiring them to do the job."

"They didn't hire them right away, though. Marvin had your *papa* give them a quote. When they made their decision, they chose the boys. They can say what they want about why they made that decision. I really believe June was drawn to them because they reminded her of their sons. I know how she would feel," Daria said, briefly laying a hand on Gaspar's arm.

Gaspar turned to his *papa* with a shrug and asked, "Why

didn't they finish the job? That doesn't seem very professional."

As Daria served him breakfast, he paused long enough to say, "Thank you, *Mama*. Did they have a time schedule and need to leave to go somewhere else?"

"No, nothing like that. Maybe your mama can answer you, but right now, I need to get some different tools," Tony said. "Gaspar, do you think you can be ready to come with me in half an hour?"

"Sure, *Papa*."

"I think this morning I may just join the two of you. June and I have been talking about a new craft we read about called macramé. You can make all sorts of things like the loveliest wall hangings or even curtains. We thought we would enjoy trying it during the long winter months. We can maybe decide on our projects today and then the next time one of us is at the store, we can ask Betty to order the kits."

Tony turned at the door and said, "Daria, that's great, but remember I told our son be ready in a half hour. Do you think you can be ready by then?"

"Well if not, I'll just walk across the street myself."

"*Mama*," Gaspar said impatiently, "You are supposed to be telling me about those guys who started the renovations for your neighbours. What did *papa* say their names were, Mark and Steve?"

"Yes, I know, but if we need to be ready in a half hour, we really don't have time to discuss it now. I suggest asking June."

Forty-five minutes later they went across the street, skirting the mud puddles that remained from last night's rain. The air hung like a cloak, raw and bitter, but at least the rain had stopped. When June opened the door, both Tony and Daria started quickly to introduce their son.

"Welcome home," June said, warmly grasping his hands in hers.

Marvin came up behind her and reached out to shake his hand. "Yes, welcome home."

Then he hastened to open the door wider. "It's chilly out. Please, come inside."

"Thank you," they chorused.

"I appreciate your greetings. It sure feels good to be back. I've enjoyed myself immensely this last week, seeing my childhood friends and being updated with news about any who have moved away. I guess you might say generally getting reacquainted with folk. But at breakfast this morning I was informed my fun is all over. I really don't mind though, after all, this was the reason for my coming home."

"Yes, and I'm not getting any closer to retirement until you get started," Tony playfully grumbled.

Which brought several smirks as everyone moved away from the door while handing Marvin their jackets. The men immediately headed upstairs. After the men left, June ushered Daria into the dining room. Soon they were browsing over the shiny pages illustrating the macramé patterns.

After awhile, June said, "I think I'll start with an easy wall hanging. I'm not good at teaching myself something new. Marvin often has to help me."

"I agree, I think it's a good idea to start with something easy. If I try something too difficult, I might need your husband's help as well."

A companionable hour had passed when Daria broke the silence. "I keep coming back to this owl. I think I'm going to have Betty order it for me."

"I've made my decision as well. I think I'll order this lovely forest glade. I need to go to the general store tomorrow, so I can place our orders. I imagine the men will be finished soon so I'd best go put the coffee on."

Daria took a minute to tidy all the magazines they had carelessly strewn across the table. She then stooped to pick up a few that had fallen onto the floor. When she had completed this task, she joined June in the kitchen.

The coffee was brewing and June was cutting a coffee cake when the men came downstairs and joined them.

"How did it go, Gaspar?" June asked him cheerily. "All ready to show up for work tomorrow?"

"Yes, Mrs. Palmer. I'll dig my painting overalls out tonight. Your husband suggested that I start on the little bedroom at the front of the house. He mentioned your daughter is coming to visit you at Thanksgiving."

"Yes, she is. I was hoping to speak to you soon about her travelling here. I understand you came on Joe's barge. That's the same way Marvin and I came when we moved here, and for that matter, all our belongings came that way, too."

"Yes, I did. I imagine it took you five nights and six days like it did when I came home," Gaspar said. "Thankfully, every day we had great weather. I know Joe told me it could even be longer if the weather is unfavourable. I'm sure you know as well as I do, the weather could make a change for the worse at any time. I really quite enjoyed my trip home, though. He has four great guys working for him, and I had a lot of fun with them."

"I can't imagine our daughter would find it very enjoyable, though. I know we came that way last summer, but..." Her voice trailed off.

"My sentiments, exactly, darling," Marvin said. "I guess one of her brothers could accompany her. Especially on her first trip here. However, we were really hoping you could suggest another way."

After Tony took a sip of his coffee he said, "You may want to give Phil a shout. I seemed to recall hearing him and Bob talk about a seaplane. It flies over from Sandspit on the Queen Charlotte Islands. I don't know the price, of course."

"June, doesn't that sound perfect? Just what we want. I don't care about the cost. I just want to be sure Shelley is safe. Thank you, Tony. I'll make a point of talking to Phil today."

As he reached for another piece of cake, Marvin said, "You girls look quite content. You must have decided on the patterns you were looking for."

"We both have. Tony, June is going to the general store tomorrow. She'll order our kits then. Can she just put it on our account?"

"Well, not if it means I have to sell my first-born son. After all, I just got him home," Tony responded with a wink to Marvin.

Everyone laughed.

Turning to face June, he said, "That will be just fine."

"You girls talking about an activity for the winter makes me think we need something as well, Marvin."

"I agree. I have often thought of wood carving. I used to like whittling simple things when I was younger."

June gave Marvin a rather surprised look before commenting, "That must have been when you were a *lot* younger. I don't think I've ever seen you whittling and I'm not aware of anything you've made."

"It was," Marvin agreed, in a tone that said he didn't want to talk about it anymore.

"In Calgary my workmates and I used to play darts," Gaspar said. "A game and laughter could sure take care of many cold, snowy evenings. We could ask Mr. Petrov if there's any place to set up a board at the Borscht Kettle."

"That sounds like a good idea," both men agreed in unison.

"Now that horseshoe season is over, I am quite sure some of the others like Phil and Frank and even Bob himself would agree," Tony said. "I'll have to mention it to Bob the next time I see him."

Tony stood then, pushing back his chair. "The morning is just about gone, Daria. Maybe we should go home, have a quick bite of lunch, then I can come back and finish the flooring."

Daria was rising to follow her husband, when Gaspar, a frown on his handsome face, suddenly blurted out, "Mrs. Palmer—"

Tony and Daria briefly looked at each other and sat down again, turning towards June.

"*Mama* said to ask you why those men you hired last summer didn't finish the job."

They all looked at each other. Then June cleared her throat, "I think all I will tell you today, Gaspar, is that Marvin and I are grateful to your *papa*, Phil, and Bob for asking them to leave town. The rest of the story, I'll tell you when Shelley comes. I am quite sure she will insist we tell her every detail. Her work is in law enforcement, so a story like this is right up her alley."

CHAPTER THREE

Planning for Shelley's Arrival

Marvin was heading to the lighthouse to see Phil Filipov, the lighthouse keeper, when he saw him walking up the street. He had a bouquet of fall flowers in his hand. Marvin smiled to himself, knowing where Phil was heading.

"Hello, Phil," Marvin called.

Phil gave a wave acknowledging Marvin, a big smile on his face, and kept on going.

"Phil, may I speak to you for a minute?"

"Oh, sure," Phil said, as he stopped and came towards him. "How are you? I don't think I've seen you or June since the weather turned cold and rainy."

"Yes, we have been keeping much closer to home since then. I don't know though if the weather has been the problem or a certain widow lady," Marvin said with a gesture towards the flowers. "I was wanting to speak to you today, though, to ask about traveling here. Our daughter Shelley plans on coming to spend Thanksgiving with us. Tony mentioned earlier this morning that you might know about a seaplane from the Queen Charlotte Islands. I gather that on request it can fly here."

Phil nodded. "You take a commercial flight from Vancouver to Sandspit via the Queen Charlotte Express. Then you can hire a partnering company called Queen Charlotte Charters to fly you anywhere within a reasonable distance. Johnny Eagle Feather is their main pilot and he operates the company. He's flown here a few times before, for various reasons. Of course, most times it was an emergency, like when Merle Rosnokov had his hunting accident. Would you like me to give him a call on the wireless and see if something can be arranged?"

"Please, Phil, and maybe ask him how much it will cost. Not that I'm concerned about that, but then I can have his cheque ready when they arrive. I'm sure Shelley will find this much more appealing than several days on a barge. I know her mother and I certainly will feel better about it. As June mentioned this morning, we really don't want to waste her vacation time with travelling."

"Sure thing. When I go home I'll give him a call. My plan is to spend the afternoon with Marg, so it might be this evening before I can let you know."

"That's fine. Thank you, Phil, I really appreciate your doing this for us," Marvin said. With a friendly slap on his back, he added, "I wouldn't want to be the reason that those flowers were wilted before you could deliver them."

"I have to agree," Phil muttered. "There aren't many flowers still blooming in the meadows—just a few black-eyed Susans, whirling butterflies and *coreopsis*. It won't be long before I won't be able to gather a bouquet that I feel is nice enough to take to her."

"Good for you, Phil. I think June has been picking them. I

kind of miss having flowers on our kitchen table. This winter she's asked me to build her a greenhouse. She figures that way she can have flowers earlier in the spring and I suppose later in the fall as well. Be sure to say hi to Marg for us and enjoy your time together."

It was almost eight o'clock that night when Phil rapped on the Palmers' door. Before he could rap again, Marvin had swung the door open.

"Come in, come in," Marvin welcomed him. "June has just brewed some decaffeinated coffee and taken some chocolate chip cookies out of the oven."

As Phil stepped inside, he lifted his head, sniffing the air and exclaiming, "Those cookies sure smell good. I just love how the chocolate oozes through my teeth when they are fresh from the oven."

Laughing, June poured him a cup of coffee as she replied, "Have as many as you like, Phil. I baked a double batch tonight."

It took no more encouragement than that for Phil to shed his brown Tweedsmuir coat and pull up a chair at the kitchen table. "Has anyone told you that Bob and Olga usually close the Borscht Kettle on the Monday of the Thanksgiving weekend? Everyone gathers at the church instead for a community social event. In the afternoon some of the young folk get together to play games, whereas we older folk usually just arrive in time for the *zakuski*." Then pausing, he added, "I think you once mentioned that what we call a *zakuski* is what you call a potluck."

"Yes, we do but no, nobody has said anything to us," June exclaimed. "What a nice idea. It certainly makes sense. It will be so much less work for Bob than if we all went to the restaurant. I also think it will be much like the atmosphere of Russia

Day. I still fondly remember what a wonderful time we had. I think I'll roast a large turkey, unless someone else is. I have one in our freezer, but maybe I should check with the other ladies first."

Marvin looked dubiously at his wife, "June, how big is the turkey, fifty pounds?"

"Oh no, not that big. I think it is maybe thirty pounds. I'd have to look at it to be certain."

"I can ask Marg, but I'm sure she might be open to cooking a turkey, instead of what she usually brings," Phil offered.

"I like that idea. That way, we could each cook a bird. With the whole village there, I'm sure the meat wouldn't go to waste. I'll have to talk to her about it."

Marvin was growing restless and finally cleared his throat, "All this talk about Thanksgiving makes my mouth water but Phil, I am most anxious to hear what you found out today. Is the flight available, or will our daughter need to come by barge?"

A big smile came across Phil's face as he said, "I managed to get a hold of Johnny. He is quite happy to fly your daughter from Sandspit. In fact, he hinted that maybe the lodge should consider flying their visitors here as an optional attraction. That gives me the idea that maybe this is something I could do in my retirement. You know, showing tourists around our village." He added with a frown, "The lighthouse is automated now."

Marvin and June unanimously heaved a sigh of relief, before June asked, "May I give Shelley a call on your wireless to let her know these arrangements?"

"For sure," Phil remarked. "Come by early tomorrow and we'll get it done."

"Did he let you know the cost?" Marvin asked.

"Yes, I wrote it down, so I wouldn't forget what he said. Here," Phil replied, as he pulled a piece of scrap paper out of his pocket and handed it to Marvin.

"That's quite the idea Johnny had about making New Petrograd a tourist attraction," June commented. "Maybe you could tour people and Anna could talk about the town's history and of course, they could have an authentic Russian meal at the Borscht Kettle. I'm sure at the end of the day any visitor would go home satisfied with their experience."

"Maybe it would give a few of us something to do. I would think the lighthouse would be a major attraction. You could be kept busy just showing it off," Marvin added.

"Yes, the idea quite appealed to me when Johnny brought it up." Before heading out into the darkened night, Phil paused a minute. "Maybe it's best if you don't say anything to Marg about how many cookies I ate."

"Our lips are sealed," June responded with a grin.

CHAPTER FOUR

Shelley's Big Day

"Hurry up, Shelley," Gordy called to his sister. "If you don't get a move on, you will miss your flight to Mom and Dad's."

"There's no way I am missing this flight! I can't wait to see Mom and Dad and I'm excited to see the village they retired to. It sounds so fascinating." Shelley's muffled voice came from her bedroom as she fastened her suitcase. She then began dragging it behind her down the hallway.

"I agree with you on the Mom and Dad part. I mean seeing them, but I don't really care about seeing the village," Gordy responded as he reached for Shelley's suitcase. "You will have to give my love to our folks though."

Lyle, Shelley's older brother, was coming through the door of Shelley's apartment just then. Upon hearing Gordy's comment, he swiftly said to Shelley, "Give them my love too. I'm really quite envious of you going to see them, Shel. You certainly have perfect weather for flying. I was a little concerned when I woke this morning and saw fog enveloping everything, but now it is an amazingly clear day. Crisp of course, but we need to remember summer is gone and autumn is beginning. Do you know how long it will take you to fly to the Queen Charlotte Islands?"

"I think the plane is what they call a twin engine, so not super fast. It will be midafternoon when I land in Sandspit. Then I transfer to the seaplane to go to the mainland. Can you imagine how awesome it will be? I'll feel like a bird suspended over the ocean."

"You're right, Lyle. It's going to be nice up there in the clouds," Gordy said.

Turning to his sister Gordy agreed with her, too, that the last leg of her flight would be fascinating.

Shelley did a final check of her apartment. She turned out the lights and the three siblings moved into the hallway. She locked the door, and they walked together to the lobby and outside to where Gordy's green Corolla was parked.

When Gordy picked up Shelley's suitcase to throw it into the trunk of his car, he turned to his sister with a grimace. "What have you packed? This suitcase weighs a ton! How long are you going for, anyway?"

"Mom advised me to pack something for every kind of weather. I've also included something for every occasion – from going fishing with Dad to a ball gown with a handsome prince," she retorted, with a twinkle in her eye. Then she bent to get into the passenger side of Gordy's vehicle.

"Good luck with finding a handsome prince in the back-woods of British Columbia," Lyle remarked. Gordy agreed as they also scrambled into the car.

"You never know where a handsome prince may be lurk-ing," she responded in a miffed voice.

As they drove down Granville Street, Lyle reiterated again how envious he was of Shelley going to visit their parents. "Tell

Mom and Dad I'm having my Thanksgiving with Mandy and her family."

"Great," Gordy said giving his brother a wry look in the rear-view mirror. "I thought we might hang out together, maybe go out for a meal. It sounds like I'm celebrating Thanksgiving by myself. I guess there'll be no turkey or pumpkin pie for me. Maybe I should try to sneak on the flight with you, Shel, and give Mom and Dad a surprise."

"Well, you know, I could always hint to Mandy that with Shelley away, you will be at loose ends," Lyle suggested. "Her parents are great people, always kind and hospitable, and her mom is a fantastic cook. I'm sure we'll have the best turkey and pumpkin pie this side of New Petrograd. I'm quite sure they would be willing to have my stranded brother over for dinner. Especially when I explain to them that I have to keep an eye on him."

Gordy gave him an appreciative smile, before saying, "Thanks, Lyle, that would be awesome. I really like Mandy. If her family is anything like her, I'm sure I'll really enjoy myself."

Then he turned his attention back to the traffic and nego-tiating the on ramp to the Oak Street bridge.

On the way to the airport, the three siblings chatted amiably on random topics. When her brothers drifted into a conversation about what was happening with the local sports teams, Shelley found herself staring, unfocused, out the window.

It took only a few moments before exiting from the bridge into Richmond. A short skip across Bridgeport Road where it joined with another bridge onto Sea Island, and they were approaching the Vancouver International Airport. Then everyone began watching for signs directing them to the South Terminal. It was Lyle who first spotted it and pointed it out.

Gordy quickly changed lanes and swung the car in that direction. He stopped by the door for Shelley and Lyle to disembark. After getting out, Lyle went around to the trunk. He waited a minute for Gordy to pop it before removing Shelley's suitcase, giving an exaggerated grunt as he did so.

With a cheery wave and "I'll catch up with you inside," Gordy drove off to look for a parking stall.

Shelley and Lyle proceeded into the terminal, scanning for the words *Queen Charlotte Express*. Upon seeing it, Shelley hastened to the counter with her ticket and ID in hand.

"Are you sure you want to go to Sandspit and not Sandpoint, my dear?" the matronly ticket agent asked. "We usually only get men travelling to Sandspit for weekly fishing trips. If you do want Sandpoint, you have come here by mistake, and you need to go to the main terminal."

Shelley hastily confirmed, "I am travelling to Sandspit. Did the travel agent issue it correctly?"

"Oh yes, everything is okay, but I still thought I would check."

Then Shelley eagerly told her about her parents retiring to a Russian village, on the mainland but across from the island. Her blue eyes sparkled with excitement when she said that someone was flying her by seaplane to New Petrograd.

The agent quickly processed everything and put her suitcase on the conveyor belt to be whisked away. Then she turned back to Shelley and handed back her ID and a boarding pass. "Enjoy your holiday with your parents," she said cheerily.

"Thank you. I will." Turning from the counter, Shelley put her ticket and boarding pass away in her purse.

When she came abreast of Lyle, she frowned and said, "Where's Gordy? He said he would meet us inside."

Lyle gave a shrug before responding, "I don't know, but I

imagine he has parked by now. My guess would be he is waiting outside. You know how crazy he is about planes and everything to do with them. We can meet him out there as well, unless you think it will be too cold."

Shelley turned with a chuckle, and answered him eagerly, "My excitement will keep me warm," and headed for the door.

When Gordy saw them coming, he shouted, "Will you get a look at that? It is a Grumman G-73 Mallard. Do you know what is so special about this plane?" After waiting a minute, and in response to Shelley and Lyle's blank stares, Gordy began, "It's an amph—"

"I know, it's flying me to see Mom and Dad," Shelley exclaimed.

Gordy looked at his sister with an expression which implied that clearly, she had lost it.

"It is an amphibious aircraft – meaning it can land both on the water or the land," he explained.

"That is a neat fact. I guess when you really look at it, it does have a boat-like shape," Lyle answered.

Seeing that a line was already forming in front of the plane's stairs, Shelley mentioned to them that maybe she should join it. Before they left her, she looked at Gordy and said, "I still think my idea was the right one."

Laughing, her brothers gave her a hug then turned and headed back towards Gordy's car.

Shelley made her way to the end of the line, appraising the other passengers as she did so. She suddenly realized they were all men. The lady at the counter had been correct. Oh well, she thought, not to worry. Being surrounded by guys is nothing new. And I've packed a couple of magazines, a *Macleans* and a *Chatelaine*, to help me pass the time.

While waiting in line she began chatting with one of the

other passengers, who she suspected was about Lyle's age. She learned his name was Brent Hoskins. He had been married five years and they had a young son, Anthony, who was three, and a baby, six months old, named Sarah. As a birthday present, his wife and his parents had given him this fishing trip. Shelley smiled to herself. She couldn't help but think how his excitement matched her own. They briefly stopped their conversation to board the plane but because there were no assigned seats they chose to sit together.

After settling into their seats, they began making small talk, and only paused chatting when Shelley heard the engines purr to life. Then she turned her attention to looking out her window as they began lifting into the skies. When the plane levelled out and she could look down onto the tops of the stark white, puffy clouds, Shelley turned her attention back to Brent and they resumed their conversation.

Brent was interested to hear about the village of New Petrograd and Shelley's pending visit with her parents. She also entertained him with some of her stories of her work as a police constable. Particularly stories that portrayed the reluctance some of the male officers showed at having women as co-workers. There didn't seem to be a lull in the conversation and when, some hours later, the plane began to bank for landing, she looked at the magazines sitting on her lap. She hadn't even opened one of them.

As Shelley was going down the stairs onto the tarmac, she noticed the air was much sharper here, cold and clear. Involuntarily, she shivered. She and Brent hurried to the small structure that served as the terminal.

Inside, the building was buzzing with activity with everyone from the flight, including the flight crew, milling around and waiting for the luggage carts. In addition, there were several drivers from local lodges. They were standing around with signs displaying the names of their anticipated guests.

Brent gathered his backpack and was walking towards the person holding up the sign with his name. Then he stopped abruptly and raced back to Shelley to shake her hand, offering well wishes for her visit. Then he was off to join the other four men standing where the driver had indicated.

In a few minutes all the commotion ceased as everyone collected their luggage and headed out the door to their waiting vehicles. Shelley was left standing in the terminal by herself. Looking around, she noticed the vending machines along one wall. Thinking it would be nice to get a coffee and possibly a sandwich, she moved across the room to stand in front of them. After observing her options, which seemed to be all the same, she put in her money to make her purchase. Just then the door briskly opened, and a large gentleman with slightly greying hair walked through it. Shelley could see the name, *Queen Charlotte Charters*, emblazoned on the front of his jacket.

She picked up her purchases and turned towards him. At the same time, he began heading her way, asking in a husky voice, "Are you Shelley Palmer?"

"Yes," she said, with a smile. "I'm assuming from the company name on your jacket you're the person who'll be flying me to New Petrograd."

"I am. Pleased to meet you. My name is Johnny Eagle Feather." He extended his hand to shake hers. "I trust you had a pleasant flight to Sandspit."

Shaking his hand, she said, "Pleased to meet you, as well. Yes, I did have a nice trip here and I'm excited about my next leg of the journey."

"Well, I hope it'll be as good as you've imagined," he replied.

He wasted no time in picking up her luggage and heading towards the door. Shelley, juggling her sandwich and coffee, fell into step beside him. When they arrived at his big, black one-ton truck, he opened the door and helped her to climb up to the seat. Then he went around to the driver's side. In just a very few minutes he parked and pointed to the plane bobbing by the dock in the marina. Shelley opened the door and quickly exited the truck, carefully carrying her coffee. Simultaneously Johnny grabbed her suitcase from the truck bed, and they started towards the plane. She walked behind him, breathing in deeply of the tangy smell of the ocean. She took note of the name painted on its tail – *Eagle Wings* – before he helped her clamber inside. *Eagle Wings* shuddered to life and as smooth as butter, they were airborne.

Shelley consumed her light lunch and then let out a huge yawn, as her eyes began to close. Some time later she awoke with a start and looked sheepishly at Johnny, apologizing for her rudeness.

"Not to worry, miss," he replied. "I imagine you're tired from your flight from Vancouver. It is good that you had a rest before tonight, as I am supposing you and your parents will visit into the wee hours. Besides, much of what we just travelled was over open ocean, but this," he offered, pointing with his hand, "is when it all gets interesting."

"I don't know about my dad, but I am sure you are right that my mom and I will stay up late talking. I have so much to tell her, and just as many questions to ask."

Looking out her window she noticed they were flying between some islands. Soon, they were nearing a cliff. It was only then she noticed with a start how the sky had become a slim line of mauve with pink clouds on the horizon. Just coming into view was a lighthouse. Her excitement started to rise as she realized he was descending in preparation for landing. Shelley could make out a cluster of miniature figures standing on the pier. As they decreased altitude, she could make out her parents among them.

"It looks like you have a welcoming committee," Johnny said, motioning towards the people gathered.

As they came up beside the dock, she said, "They are not all for me. The dark-haired lady in the beige duffel coat is my mom and the grey-haired man in navy blue Dockers and a grey jacket is my dad."

Then she erupted into gales of laughter as she caught her mother's expression as the wharf rocked from the swell the *Eagle Wings* created when it landed in the water. Then her mother was exuberantly waving to her and she was waving back.

Shelley could hardly contain herself as Johnny fastened the seaplane to the dock. Upon making sure it was secure, he opened the door of the cabin and offered her a hand out. Marvin quickly came to offer his assistance and gave her a huge hug and greeted her with, "Welcome to our new home, my love."

Letting go of her, he hastily moved to collect her luggage from Johnny, who was exclaiming, "Have a wonderful visit, see you in nine days. Thank you," he then said to Marvin, as he received the cheque in payment.

Her mother was now disentangling herself from the other women and she raced over. Looking Johnny in the eye, she offered a heartfelt, "Thank you for bringing her safely here," while protectively wrapping her arm around Shelley.

June turned back to the other people and said, "Olga, I

sure hope everything goes well. Uri, our thoughts will be with you and Anna." Then with Shelley sandwiched between her parents, they began walking towards the village.

Once they were safely across the street from the pier Shelley paused to look back, noticing the tall, husky man was speaking to Johnny Eagle Feather. Then he was helping the younger woman, who, she realized with surprise, was very pregnant, into the plane. Then the husky man was also getting ready to board the plane.

As they entered the main street of the village they stepped onto a lit boardwalk in front of a few stores, which were all closed for the day except for the one at the corner. She noticed with delight it was called the Borscht Kettle. Marvin took a step back, allowing June and Shelley to walk in front of him.

"Oh, what fun," Shelley cried. "It's just like a frontier town with this boardwalk." She then hooked her arm in June's and said, "Mom, I thought you told me that Dad had hired the seaplane to bring me here. So, I'm very surprised and curious about why Johnny Eagle Feather has passengers going back."

"Yes, that was a sudden decision made this afternoon. They decided to fly Anna and her husband Uri to Sandspit. Anna is about eight months pregnant. Her blood pressure keeps rising so Miss Montgomery, the district nurse, thought it best for her to see a doctor. We're between the hospital in Sandspit and the one in Prince Rupert. It was very convenient that you were flying here today so they could take advantage of the return flight. I know Anna is very disappointed, because she wanted a midwife to deliver her baby at home. Since moving here, Anna's parents, Bob and Olga Petrov, have become some of our special friends. They own the Borscht Kettle, the restaurant and pub. You may have noticed it on the corner when we crossed the street. Olga has invited us there one night for a lovely Russian meal."

Shelley looked at her mother, concern written on her face. "Oh, I hope everything will be all right with the baby, and yes, I did notice the Borscht Kettle and was tickled by the name."

By now they had reached the end of the boardwalk, and Marvin stepped closer, so he could again take hold of his daughter's arm, helping her to step down.

As she regained her footing on the pathway, Shelley let out a little yelp of shock, as she realized they were now in complete darkness. Even in the dark she was aware of her parents' shoulders shaking in mirth. Then Marvin casually pulled a flashlight out of his jacket pocket and turned it on, handing it to June.

Her mom said, "Yes, some things are a little different here. The warmth Dad and I received from all the residents when we moved here last summer was most welcoming. Especially considering it could have been so different. Hardly anyone has moved here since it was originally settled after the Russian revolution. It will only take a few more minutes now and we will be home. I have a light supper waiting and you can tell us about your flight here. Then we can get into a more serious conversation. I am so anxious to catch up on all the news from home. Specifically, anything you can share about your brothers who, I might add, are not very good at corresponding."

CHAPTER FIVE

Meeting Shelley

Tony was sitting enjoying a roaring fire crackling in the fire-place one miserable, rainy afternoon. He was casually looking at a brochure on cruises that Daria had not so subtly put in his hand. When he was feeling tired, he put the brochure down, reclined his easy chair, and was promptly snoring.

Daria came in shortly after and, nudging him awake, offered him a cup of coffee and a plate of her fresh baking. "Well, dear, how are you enjoying your first full day of retirement?" she kindly asked as she sat down on the couch opposite.

"I sure am. Do you have any idea what it feels like to be lazing in the middle of the afternoon on a weekday?"

"I have no idea." Daria laughed. "You know the old saying, *A man can work from sun to sun, but a woman's work is never done.* That's why I gave you the brochure about cruises. I thought it would be something nice for us to consider now."

Tony cleared his throat, before sheepishly remarking, "I must admit that I hardly looked at it."

"Hmph," Daria replied. "I'll have to ask June if she had any more luck with Marvin."

"Is June in on this cruise idea, too?"

"Yes, she is. Betty ordered us brochures from a few different cruise lines."

Tony let out a groan, before staring thoughtfully at his wife and hesitantly asking, "Is Betty in on this scheme as well?"

"Yes," Daria casually answered, as she bent to pick up Tony's empty coffee cup.

However, Tony quickly blocked her hand, so she was forced to look at him. "And just who else?"

"Olga. Now I need to hurry and put the finishing touches on a salad. We have been invited to June's for dinner tonight, as she'd like us to meet their daughter. I told her I would bring the salad. Where is Gaspar? He's been invited as well, and I'd like him to come."

"He went to Marg Rosnokova's to give her a quote on some work she'd like done," Tony told her.

Daria stopped and turned back to look at Tony, noticing with a smile he had picked up the brochure again. "I don't think Marg ever had you do anything at her house. It just makes me wonder, is she anticipating wedding bells soon?"

Tony shook his head, exclaiming, "Daria, you think too much! Wedding bells... really. You're right, though, that I never did any renovations for her and Merle. I think he or their sons could repair or renovate anything. In fact, Merle often used to ask me for my advice on how to do things. I assume that, in the five years since she's been widowed, perhaps she hasn't felt like doing anything. I took it to be an indication she is getting over her grieving for Merle."

"That may be the case but, you mark my words, in the end you'll see who's right."

Not long after that they heard the back door open. Gaspar came in, shaking his head and saying, "It is pouring outside like I've never seen before!"

Tony let out a chuckle, looking at his son. "Guess the prairies have made you soft, my boy."

Gaspar bent to remove his galoshes. "I have to admit, *Papa*, the prairies can sure get cold, but it's different because it's a dry cold. It doesn't seep into your bones like this does."

"Gaspar," Daria cut in before her son could leave the room, "we've been invited to our neighbours, the Palmers, for supper tonight."

"That's okay, Mom. I'll just finish the lasagne you made last night."

"First of all, Gaspar, there are no leftovers. *Papa* and I had them for lunch today. Second, June has planned this dinner because she wants us to meet their daughter."

"Gee, *Mama*—" Gaspar started to say.

Tony spoke up. "Gaspar, you've got to start thinking from the perspective that the people in the village are your potential customers. Showing friendliness with them is just one of the things you need to do."

"I understand what you are telling me about the village folk and that may be true. What I want to know is, what has some girl from Vancouver got to do with that?"

Daria quickly moved across the kitchen, and wrapping her son in a bear hug, commented, "It seems to me her *mama* promised to tell you something when her daughter came."

Gaspar's eyes lit up and he nodded as realization dawned. "Yes, that's true."

Tony, with a nod of approval to his wife, said, "And that is what a girl from Vancouver has to do with your business."

"Okay. I'll go change and get ready."

"I'm pleased that you've agreed to come. I know June is expecting you and she'll be disappointed if you don't. I don't expect you to stay all evening, dear, if you really don't want to," Daria called to his retreating back.

———

"That was sure good, Mrs. Palmer," Gaspar said as June removed his dinner plate.

Giving him a pleased smile, June said, "My husband can cut some more ham. I have more scalloped potatoes and vegetables, if you like."

"Oh no, I'm stuffed," Gaspar said, as he stretched back in his chair.

As June reached for each individual dinner plate, she received similar compliments and groans from her other guests.

Shelley, who had sat quietly listening throughout much of the meal, stood then. "I helped Mom bake a chocolate cake this afternoon."

"Well, bring it in, then," Marvin said with a smile to his daughter and wife. "I'm sure you could use a piece as well, Tony, Gaspar?" Then he added, "I understand today is quite important, Gaspar, being the first day you are taking over from your dad. What did I hear him say last week, that he had been doing the village's renovations for thirty-five years?"

"That is correct," Tony confirmed. "It sure felt good to be relaxing in my easy chair all day. Especially with the weather we had today."

As everyone finished their dessert, Shelley picked up her teacup. "Mom, you said when I came that you would tell me about those guys you hired last summer, and you haven't said anything about them yet."

Gaspar perked up, looking first at Shelley then back at June with an expectant expression.

"I did," June said. "I told both you and Gaspar I would. I guess with both of you here tonight I shouldn't put it off any longer."

As everyone settled in their seats, she smiled, then began, "Please feel free to interrupt me – it isn't just Marvin's and my story any longer. I believe it's a part of New Petrograd's recent history.

"One night in the summer, we had everyone here for a potluck. We really hadn't thought much about how long the boys were taking to do the work. However, we had set the date thinking it would be complete by then. It was a lovely summer evening, so we spent most of it in the backyard."

Marvin interjected, "We menfolk enjoyed playing horse-shoes all evening. There weren't even bugs out that night. I don't think I can recall any of us swatting at a fly, much less anything else."

"That is correct. We ladies noticed it also when we were sitting and visiting. When there were just a few people left at the end of the evening, I mentioned to them I would invite everyone in, but our hardwood flooring wasn't finished yet."

Tony picked up the story. "I asked if I could see how things were going." Then he proceeded to tell them of his shock when he looked in the room and saw all they had done was to rip up the old flooring. They hadn't even begun to lay the new hardwood.

Daria looked at Gaspar. "*Papa* let out a string of Italian. I wasn't even in the room yet, but I knew that didn't sound like good news."

Gaspar put back his head, and roared with laughter. "A string of my *papa*'s Italian used to mean I had better run."

As the laughter around the table petered out, June continued, "The next morning several of the men gathered here to discuss the situation with Mark and Steve. Bob Petrov put on his sheriff's hat and asked a few questions and things turned very sour quickly. He then mentioned that although he felt they hadn't done anything that was considered illegal, it might be in everyone's best interests if they left the village. Bob and Phil escorted them back to their boat and watched as they set sail."

June finished by saying, "That is perhaps a short version, but I have included the most important details. We had really enjoyed having the boys working here, so we were very sorry it ended on an unpleasant note. Now," she said as she got up, "does anyone else want anything more to eat?"

Shelley asked, "Is the Bob Petrov you speak of the same man who is the proprietor of the Borscht Kettle you told me about the other night?"

"Yes," Marvin answered. "Why are you asking, dear?"

"I guess it just seems different having him as a sheriff as well. Then again, if there are only one hundred people living here, it shouldn't surprise me that you don't have full-time law enforcement."

There were several nods of agreement around the room, before Marvin responded, "After Vancouver and you and your workmates, it's probably a welcome change for you." He added with a caustic smile at the corner of his mouth, "We would be a part of the only incident this village has witnessed in years, probably decades."

Shelley thought about what her dad said, before turning back to her mom. "Is that all there is to the story? I think you wrote me something about the boys' real purpose being to look for hidden jewels here."

Gaspar looked at Shelley, taking notice of her long blonde hair. She was really a pretty girl. Then he turned to look at her *mama* with a quizzical expression.

Marvin crossed his legs the other way, suggesting he thought he would be sitting for a while longer. Looking at his wife with an amused expression, he said, "Didn't you tell Gaspar earlier that Shelley would want every detail? I think that has just happened!"

"I did," June said, playfully frowning at her daughter. "I guess these dishes can wait a while longer." She then continued, "This is a part of our family's history."

"I can start cleaning up, Mom," Shelley offered. "I can do the dishes and still listen."

"Would you like some help? I can dry the dishes," Gaspar said, moving his chair back from the table.

"Sure," Shelley replied, briefly lifting her head in acknowledgement of his offer. Then she turned her attention back to picking up dessert dishes and making her way to the sink.

Once more, June began to speak, "This is a story of my family. My *babushka*, Elena Bolitchnova, and my Great Aunt Tatyana Feodociv were working as confidantes in the Russian court before the revolution. Tensions were high in Russia and the royal family felt it best to send several of their employees out of the country with their jewels. They hid the jewels by sewing them into their undergarments, or the hems of their clothing. Some of the men had jewels sewn into the linings of their hats.

"Many of these people were caught and killed leaving Russia. Sadly, my *dedushka* Bolitchnov was one of the people killed so I never knew him. Great Aunt Tatyana and *babushka* Elena, with baby Margarita, who was my mother, made it safely to London. From there they sailed to the new world, and a new life in this seemingly strange land. On the ship coming over, Great Aunt Tatyana met and fell in love with Yarostav Pagodon. They were married soon after they landed in Halifax. Then Great Aunt Tatyana and her new husband travelled west to start their life as a married couple. There they joined other Russian immigrants coming to New Petrograd, making them some of New Petrograd's founding fathers. Sadly, they were never blessed with children.

"When my great aunt was near death, she confided in my mother, who was by then her only living relative, about the jewels she had escaped from Russia with, hidden in her coat. We know from history that all the Russian royal family was shot and so she and her husband kept the jewels. These jewels were now hidden in their home. That was the only information my mother got, because my great aunt was not able to communicate any more.

"So, through the years, I kept watching for this house to go on the market and when it did, we purchased it for our retirement. Since moving in I, too, have been on the search for the jewels. One day I came home from picking wildflowers and was going in the front door when I caught a glimpse of something strange about the doorknob. I went back later to investigate, never expecting the jewels, but there they were and once disturbed, they all came tumbling out. My hands couldn't catch them all and some spilled onto the verandah. They had been hidden for I can only guess how many years in the front doorknob.

"Now, Shelley, I believe there was a link between the boys and the jewels. On Russia Day we learned Mark's surname and it was the same as my great aunt's. It makes me wonder if his family were long-lost relatives of Tatyana."

Shelley and Gaspar had stopped working and had turned from the sink to stare at June. When she finished, Shelley said, "Wow, Mom, that is wild, even for me."

Gaspar let out a low whistle, "Thank you, Mrs. Palmer, for sharing everything. That is some tale."

"It runs shivers down my back, just listening to it again," Daria said.

"It sure does," Tony agreed.

"Thank you, honey, for telling it again," Marvin said, smiling at his wife. "Shelley, before you get any wild ideas about your parents' huge inheritance, your mother and I have already decided that we'd like to donate the money we received from the Royal BC Museum to do things around the village, wherever they feel the money will be needed the most.

"Now, I think everyone has finished telling stories. So, if those dishes are done, is anyone interested in a table game?"

"I've got just a couple of pots left to wash, and we'll be finished. Just so you know, Mom and Dad, I am proud of your plans to offer the money to the village. I know Lyle will agree, and Gordy might be a case, but I'm sure the rest of us can talk him around eventually."

"You're right, Shelley. We'll leave the handling of your brother to you," Marvin laughingly retorted.

Shelley and June hooted, joining in the family joke, which brought smiles from their guests.

Then, giving Gaspar a flicker of a smile, Shelley turned back to the sink.

Before picking anything up from the draining board, Gaspar asked, "Do you have a crokinole game, Mr. Palmer?"

"I sure do. It's in the spare bedroom that Shelley is using."

Marvin said, as he got up from the table. "Shelley, do you mind me going into your room?"

"Not at all. Dad, just a word of caution, though. It may be messy." She gave Gaspar another brief smile as she said, "It's a game I enjoy playing as well."

"Bring out a bunch of our games," June called, as he left the room. She then began to prepare a spot on the table for the crokinole board.

Daria looked quickly at Gaspar's back. She then glanced at Tony, a slow smile starting to form.

CHAPTER SIX

Vacation Week

"I can't believe how fast the days are going," Shelley said Friday morning as she wandered into the kitchen. Coming up behind her dad, she enveloped him in a huge hug.

"Yes," Marvin said patting her hands. "Tonight is another big night, a tradition here. It's fish and chips night at the Borscht Kettle. We won't stay long, though, because we need to come home and prepare for tomorrow's fishing trip. Phil is going to take us to a nearby river. I don't recall the name, but that doesn't matter."

"We sure have enjoyed showing you this village and introducing you to the lovely folks who have become our friends," June said, as she handed her daughter a huge mug of coffee and set a breakfast of toast and jam at a place setting. "Would you also like some sausage and eggs, honey?"

Crossing one leg under her as she sat down, Shelley exclaimed, "No thanks, Mom. I didn't come here for you to fatten me up. I have to say it feels like every day of my time here has been my favourite day."

Reaching for the cream to add to her coffee, she continued,

"It was wonderful to have that first weekend to sleep in and poke about your lovely, cozy home when I first arrived. I finally had time to look at the magazines I bought to read on my flight here. Then, Monday evening, I really enjoyed it when your neighbours Mr. and Mrs. Rosso and their son Gaspar came for supper. I appreciated it so much, Mom, when you told me about your experience with Mark and Steve, including the real reason for them wanting to do the renovations. You also divulged some of our family history that I knew nothing about.

"Then, on Tuesday, there was the crisp walk we took around the village, kicking up the crunchy brown and yellow autumn leaves. I was very touched when we stopped in front of the old church and read the plaque displaying the names of the founding fathers. It sent a thrill through me to see your great aunt and uncle's names. It may sound strange, but a rush of pride went through me and I really felt a sense of belonging here."

On the plaque was written:

This plaque is in memory of the first settlers of New Petrograd who came to the Dominion of Canada after fleeing the Russian Revolution of 1917.

Pyotr Rosnokov and Nadeshda Rosnokova
Roman Molodtsov and Katerina Molodtsova
Pyotr Filipov and Elena Filipova
Vasily Filipov and Tatyana Filipova
Yaroslav Pagodonov and Tatyana Pagodonova
Alexander Yusporov and Anastasia Yusporova
Pavel Katovik and Yulia Katovik
Nikolai Petrov and Margarita Petrova

Mitslav Golubov and Olesia Golubova

FOUNDERS OF NEW PETROGRAD

June cut into her daughter's musings. "The plaque has always been a very special spot for me. When it was pleasant weather, Dad and I often take an evening walk past it. I also loved the meadows that I used to wander through while Dad was fishing. I really enjoyed picking the many gorgeous wildflowers that grew there. Then Dad and I often ended our day with a meal at the Borscht Kettle."

"I sure enjoyed my Russian meal of borscht soup, rye bread, and a hot tea when we stopped there. It warmed up my insides on such a chilly day."

"If you enjoyed that, just wait for tonight," Marvin said, with exuberance.

"Then on Wednesday, we strolled back to the pier so I could get some pictures of the lighthouse. It was fabulous that Mr. Filipov invited us in, so I could get photos not just of the exterior but of the view looking out from inside. It was breathtaking, especially observing the dark storm clouds moving like demons towards the land. From that viewpoint you feel like you're a part of them."

"We were lucky." June grinned at her daughter. "I'm really glad we caught him when we did. Now that the lighthouse has been automated, I'm quite sure most of his time is spent with Marg at her place."

"Luck seemed to be with us the entire day," Marvin said. "It was spellbinding to have a bird's eye view of those huge black storm clouds moving so threateningly across the sky. Yet by the time they unleashed buckets of rain, we were sitting at John Petrov's kiosk. Nothing like sitting out a storm while enjoying a hot chocolate and chat with him. Of course, that is a risky business, because one never knows how long a storm will last."

"You are right, Dad; the torrent stopped just long enough for us to cross the street and make our way to the general store. I was so amused at the boardwalk when I arrived. Remember I called it a frontier town? Then when I stepped into the store, I truly felt like I entered one of my childhood storybooks. It was like a step back in time. I know the store isn't big, but every inch of space was being used, with every imaginable item. Mr. and Mrs. Yusporov seemed to fit my image of the proprietors as well.

"Then we finished our ramble with a visit to Christella Katovik's hairdressing shop. Who would have thought the ladies of New Petrograd had so much to talk about! I enjoyed listening to them. Of course, they mostly spoke about the pending arrival of Anna's baby. Mrs. Petrov mentioned the doctor wanted to keep her in Sandspit on bed rest until the baby is born. It sounded like the doctor thought perhaps it might arrive prematurely. Several ladies were busy knitting for the new arrival. Then there were conversations on books or crafts like this new one, macramé. That really surprised me, that the ladies of a remote village would know about it, because it is all the rage in Vancouver."

"Now, we're not so remote that we don't have magazines," June replied, with a grin. "Mrs. Rosso and I recently ordered kits. In fact, I should have thought to ask Betty if they had come when we were there Tuesday."

Marvin noted, "I stopped and saw Paul Katovik to have my hair cut while you ladies saw Christella. My haircut didn't take very long and that was when I raced back to visit Phil to discuss tomorrow's fishing trip. Phil sounds like he has everything arranged. He'll borrow Merle's truck so I can drive us through the bush to the river."

"Don't be too long fishing," June warned. "Remember the next day is Sunday and I am so anticipating Father Nikolas's sermon. I expect it will be on Thanksgiving."

"Then yesterday Mr. and Mrs. Yusporov had us for supper with their son Alex and their daughter-in-law Anna. I was entranced as Anna told me about the village forefathers' trek across Russia to England... of the fears they faced each day... eventually making their way into London. How they boarded a steamer and sailed across the Atlantic to Halifax. She told of how, when they arrived, they had bent to kiss the Canadian soil with tears in their eyes. Of how, when they spoke to the immigration people, they were told of homesteading land in the west. That's how they ended up on this rocky outcrop in the Pacific Northwest.

"I loved how Anna's eyes lit up when she finished by saying, 'And to think many of us are now a part of this story. Even your *roditeli* moving here are now part of the town's history. They've fit in so well, and we all love having them here'."

Friday evening, despite the rain which had fallen all day, the Palmers got out their umbrellas and made their way to the Borscht Kettle as soon as it was getting dark. Already, much to Shelley's amazement, the place was full, and they needed to wait for a table. They stood just inside the door and Shelley couldn't help but notice how everyone warmly greeted her parents, who then proudly introduced her. It left her with a lovely warm feeling inside, although a very sore hand from all the handshaking. She noticed that people left soon after they finished eating. She was glad because just watching the huge platters of battered fish and fries being served was leaving her stomach grumbling. When a table for six came available, her parents quickly invited Phil and Marg to join them.

They hadn't been sitting at the table long when Marvin patted Phil on the back and said to Shelley, "These are probably two of the best people to tell you the history of fish and chips night. Marg is Bob's sister. It was their *roditeli* who started this tradition."

So, between mouthfuls, Marg told of her *papa's* foresight in planning an evening at the end of each week when everyone could gather in the modest restaurant he had opened.

Phil broke in to the conversation to say, "Bob and Marg's *papa* didn't want a fancy meal. He wanted one that the children would also enjoy, so he established a menu of fish – which was always easily available. Fries and ice cream seemed to compliment the fish. I believe what my Uncle Nikolai and Aunt Margarita wanted most was family time."

Marg heartily agreed.

Marg shared that in the early days her *mama* would make the ice cream. "Whereas now, you see, my lazy brother just orders it through Frank and Betty," she finished with a cheeky grin, as Bob leaned over to serve their dessert.

That brought huge guffaws from everyone in earshot. Then they all sat back to enjoy the rest of their meal.

CHAPTER SEVEN

Thanksgiving Day

June went quietly about her kitchen, cheerily humming a line from "Over the River and Through the Woods" to herself as she prepared everything for the potluck. She had dressed the turkey and got it in the oven very early and was now doing the dishes.

"Mom, what time did you get up this morning?" Shelley came into the kitchen rubbing her eyes.

June stopped long enough to turn and face her daughter and said, "Oh, not too early. This bird is only thirty pounds, so it just needs five to six hours. I put it in early enough that it will be ready by the time we need to leave."

"Sit down and have a cup of tea, Mom. I'll finish whatever you still need done. You can give me instructions while you relax," Shelley said as she pulled out a chair for June. Then she held out her hand to take the cup her mother was about to wash.

"I will appreciate a break for sure, but other than washing these few dishes and putting everything away, I'm almost done.

I don't have to do anything with the meat. Your father will slice it at the church."

Marvin came in, towing a wagon behind him. Hearing June's comment he nodded in agreement. "I found this wagon in the garden shed. Just look at it. I believe it may be a real antique. It had a broken wheel, but I gave it a quick fix and I think it'll be just what I need to haul the turkey. I don't relish the idea of carrying a hot turkey in my hands. Is Marg cooking one also, June?"

"No, I spoke to her when we were at the hairdressers on Wednesday. She had already bought the ingredients to make an Olivier salad. It seems it has been a longstanding tradition for her to bring it to the Thanksgiving potluck. I sure wasn't going to discourage her, knowing how delicious that salad is." Turning back to Shelley, she explained, "It's the Russian version of potato salad."

June continued by saying, "I found it interesting the other day when the ladies at Christella's told us of the history of Thanksgiving in New Petrograd. It seems it has been a tradition since Miss Green introduced them to the Canadian holiday. I understand she was the district nurse here when some of them were children, Marg mentioned how everyone in the village's *roditeli* always celebrated it. She expressed that their forefathers had known a deep thankfulness for their safety in this new land."

Shelley told her mother how much she was looking forward to visiting some more with the village people today. "Plus," she added, "partaking of traditional Russian dishes."

———

Phil walked through the cold, grey morning towards Marg's house. It was more than just chilly—Jack Frost had paid a visit last night. When he arrived at Marg's he was more than ready to step into her warm kitchen. He was even more ready to step into her warm embrace.

"I think I have everything ready to go, honey. I'd like to get to the church in good time as I know it will get packed quickly."

Phil stepped forward to peek into the box, where he saw a huge bowl of salad. "I'll take care of this."

Marg stopped what she was doing abruptly, and turning with a jaunty lift of her head, said, "Just what does 'taking care of it' mean?"

Phil put the box under one arm, while reaching for Marg's hand. "It means, I'll carry it for you! Be sure to put on your warmest coat. I can feel winter's bite in the wind today."

"Oh my, I should have thought of that earlier," Marg answered. Taking a swift glance at the wall calendar, she noted, "After all, it is October eighth. I'll need to dig my winter coat out of the spare closet."

Phil carefully laid down the box on the counter before offering to help her. "I'd bring out everything—toque, scarf, gloves—if I were you. I had to tuck my hands inside my pockets on the way over to keep them warm."

"Thank you, Phil. I imagine you are right. We'll need all this extra clothing until the warm spring rains return. I'm pretty sure that I know where I put everything away, so it'll probably be quickest for me to get them myself."

In just a few minutes Marg came back to the kitchen with her light blue duffel coat and matching scarf and toque on. She was still struggling to put on her black leather gloves, though. Phil reached to help her, ending with a light kiss on her hand.

Then he again picked up the box with everything Marg had packed, and they headed for the church.

———

"Bob," Olga was saying. "I've packed dishes for ourselves and our guests. I'm thinking you may want to stop at our restaurant and bring a few more. I did try to remind all the women to bring enough for their whole family, but every year it seems that someone forgets something."

"Well let's make sure it isn't you. I know organizing this event means a lot is on your mind, but if I had to do it, well then, it would be on my mind," Bob said, ducking out of the way of the dishtowel Olga was swatting playfully in his direction. "Did you remember to tell June? This is their first Thanksgiving here."

"Yes, I made a mental note, but it was only last Friday, when they came for fish and chips, that I remembered to tell her," Olga divulged sheepishly. "Thankfully, Phil had already let them know. She's planning to bring a turkey as she had one on hand."

"Sounds delicious. I'll also get a few serving utensils. I ordered in lots of napkins from Frank, but I suggested he just bring them when they come."

Looking at the clock, Bob realized with a start that they needed to finish getting everything together and leave.

"I hear a nasty wind picking up outside, so I'm glad we've dressed warm. It isn't rainy, so we have to be thankful for small mercies," Bob commented. Then they stepped outside, and briskly walked away from their house.

"Well I sure hope between now and supper you find a few more things to be thankful for," Olga said, with a smile.

———————

Around four in the afternoon people began to gather. As they came in sight of the church, the air began to ring with greetings.

"Hello!"

"Happy Thanksgiving!"

Then they stepped into the welcome warmth of the church. Once inside it was necessary to make their way past the pews and go into the large meeting room at the back.

Gaspar and Martin were busy with a game of chess while others sat around watching. In another corner several were gathered just chatting, gales of laughter arising. Especially from Gayle, whose high-pitched peals rose above the others. Still another group were gathered around a table playing another game.

Upon seeing folks arriving with their arms laden, Gaspar got up and clapped his hands to call everyone to order. The church danced with activity while the men set up several long tables in the middle of the room. Then it was the women's turn as they got busy placing their dishes on the tables, their brightly coloured dresses swirling as they bustled.

June stopped working long enough to face Shelley. "Oh Shel, it is just like I thought, like Russia Day! Well, not exactly, because that was outdoors, of course, but the atmosphere, I mean."

The men were by now arranging the tables and chairs for everyone to sit while enjoying their meal.

When the frenzied activity died down, Tony looked around and commented thoughtfully, "You know, I don't think Bob and Olga are here. Has anyone seen them?"

There was a chorus of "No, come to think of it, I haven't seen them either," as people started to look around.

"Jenny and I thought we saw them earlier, going into their restaurant," Nick Kutuz reported.

"Did you see them come out?" Tony asked.

"Well, no but I have to admit, I guess I didn't think that much about it."

"This seems very unlike them. They're usually not late," Tony remarked.

"Oh my," Marg said, "what if one of them had an accident in there?"

"Well, at least Bob had me bring the napkins," Frank said, while Betty turned to him with a disgusted look.

"Frank really, as if that actually matters. Be serious for once. Something may have happened to them."

"What do you think, John? Should we go have a look for your *roditeli*?" Gaspar asked.

"I don't know, maybe." John replied with a worried look.

Several of the men had begun putting on their jackets and were heading for the door when Marvin, who was standing just inside the hall, said, "I think I heard the door open. Maybe that's them now."

Sure enough, they could see Bob and Olga making their way past the rows of pews. There were also three other people a few feet behind them, still in the shadows. As they drew nearer, everyone realized it was Anna and Uri, and another man.

Heads turned in disbelief and a collective gasp went up as everyone comprehended that the newcomers were holding a baby. Then the whole congregation erupted into a commotion.

"Oh Anna, congratulations, congratulations," Marg said, as she rushed forward towing Phil behind her. Phil's mind was flashing back, remembering when his own twin girls were born. For just a second, he thought so vividly, with a stab of emotion, of his wife, Millie.

Anna spoke then. "We'd like to introduce you all to our son Matthew and Uri is holding our daughter Madeline. They are quite premature but these two couldn't wait to meet us. They're so tiny. Matthew was just six pounds four ounces, and Madeline four pounds twelve ounces."

As Anna was speaking, Uri snuggled Madeline closer to his chest, giving a kiss on her brow. Then exclaimed, "Oh, Anna, we have them wrapped in the wrong colour blanket."

Which caused another uproar as everyone broke out in laughter. Although for some of the men it sounded more like snickering.

As the laughter died down, Olga said, "We have one more guest," and beckoned to the third newcomer. "For those of you who haven't met him before, this is Johnny Eagle Feather, the pilot who flies between here and Sandspit."

This time the room erupted into clapping. Which caused Johnny to look down to hide his flushing.

Anna quickly said, "Seeing this is Monday and we understand Shelley is flying to Sandspit tomorrow afternoon, we suggested he stay over tonight rather than going back and forth."

"Oh, please don't remind me I have to go home tomorrow!" Shelley wailed. "I am so thankful for my vacation at Mom and Dad's. I've so enjoyed meeting everyone this week."

Bob then spoke up, in a voice gruff with emotion, and wrapping his arms around Olga, said, "Regardless of the colour of their blankets, they are one hundred percent precious, or should I say two hundred percent precious. We are so excited to welcome Matthew and Madeline to our family." Then his smile grew into the biggest of smiles as he reached to take Matthew from Anna.

Afterwards, Father Nikolas spoke. "Well perhaps if that is all the surprises for today, we could bow our heads and give thanks. Then after dinner, perhaps everyone could share a word about what they feel thankful for."

June and Marvin led Shelley down the *zakuski* table, telling her the names of all the dishes that by now seemed familiar to them. There was *blini* – a Russian version of a pancake; *golubtsy* – very similar to cabbage rolls; Olivier salad – a potato salad; lasagne; *kissel* – a gelatin fruit dessert; and *sharlotka* cake – a cake made with Granny Smith apples for dessert. There was another salad which they didn't know, and Gayle told them it was called *mimosa* – a tunafish salad. Of course, there was also June's turkey and stuffing. Sprinkled among the main course dishes were a myriad of condiments. When June, Marvin, and Shelley had filled their plates from the generous selection, they joined a table where Daria and Tony were already seated.

Shelley was very disappointed that Gaspar wasn't sitting with his parents and subtly tried looking around the by now overflowing room for his dark head. She didn't see him sitting anywhere. Had he left already?

She was aware suddenly she had let her mind wander and had just refocused when she heard her dad say to Mr. Rosso, "I think us men are sunk, with all the women ganging up and talking about a cruise."

Then came her mother's exasperated response, "Marvin, I don't think you should use *sunk* and *cruise* in the same sentence. Those words just don't go together." June smiled as those who had heard her comment chuckled.

As everyone finished eating and were settling back in their

chairs with a beverage, Uri stood to speak first. "I am thankful for the safe arrival of my babies. My wife was a trooper."

Anna followed him by saying, "I am thankful for my babies as well, but also that my wonderful husband was by my side."

Shelley's attention was diverted from what Anna was saying as she realized with a start that someone was standing behind her, tapping on her shoulder.

"Shelley, would you care to join me and some of my friends?" Gaspar then looked towards Marvin. "Don't worry, sir, I'll walk her home when it is time to leave."

With their backs turned as they walked away, all four parents glanced at each other and smiled with approval.

Betty was expressing her thanks for safety and good food to eat all year while Gaspar led Shelley back to where his friends were sitting. Gaspar took a minute to introduce Shelley to the Shatrovs and their daughter Angela, who was sitting on her *mama's* lap, and Alexander Bolitchyn and his sister Alexandria.

Then, while he was still standing, he expressed how thankful he was that he had had a safe trip home, and almost as an afterthought as he began to sit down, he added, "And my mama's cooking." This brought a lot of snickers as several people turned to smile at Daria.

Gayle passed Angela to Martin and boldly stood up. "I am thankful Martin is a good husband and provider."

Making a great display, Alexander cockily stood, and said, "How thankful I am that Mrs. Petrov was a good teacher." Those sitting nearby saw Alexandria give him a playful swat. Alexander was just about to retaliate but caught a look from his *mama* and didn't.

Alexandria popped up after him. "I'm also thankful Mrs.

Petrov is a good teacher." Looking pointedly at her brother and then Olga she added, "And I mean it."

To which Olga playfully shook her finger at them and responded, "I'll catch you both at school tomorrow."

Dedushka Alexander Yusporov, the last remaining founding father, stood and shakily leaned on his cane, while Frank supported him. He croaked out his thankfulness for the safety they had found in this new land.

Marvin and June stood together and with their arms around each other, June expressed their thankfulness for the warmth and kind friendships they had found in New Petrograd. As if deep in thought, Marvin said, "I am thankful for everything—for living in New Petrograd, for living so close to nature, for family and friends."

When he sat down, a murmur of "I agree," rose from several in the gathering.

One by one, all the village folk stood and uttered a word of what they were most thankful for. Even little Maria Katovik offered her thanks, saying to everyone's amusement, "I am thankful for two more playmates."

Finally, Johnny Eagle Feather shyly stood and expressed his thankfulness for the amazing meal he had just partaken of. Turning his gaze upon Bob and Olga, he added, "I'm also thankful for the warm bed I have been promised for tonight."

As Shelley and Gaspar made their way home through the starlit night, Shelley gave Gaspar a sideways glance and her breath caught in her throat. He really was handsome and so gallant, making sure her coat was warm enough and taking her hand to ensure she didn't stumble on the rough, uneven patches. Turning to him in the dark, as the moon lit their faces, she breathlessly said, "Today has been such a magical climax to my vacation."

CHAPTER EIGHT

Life Goes On

Gaspar was making his way to the Borscht Kettle on Tuesday afternoon to meet some of the young folk from the village. He glanced up to see a seaplane rise into the skies and his heart took a nose dive. For the rest of his walk, all he could think was, *She's gone*.

Stepping inside the Kettle, he saw where the others were seated, and after asking Bob for a *medovukha*, crossed the room to join them.

He had been sitting at the table for a half hour, only smiling wryly at the others' gales of laughter, or making the odd comment, when Alexander slapped his leg and said, "Where are you, Gaspar? At the bottom of the sea?"

"More like up in the skies," offered Alex, grinning at Gaspar. "Let's all get focused, though. No more idle chatter."

Anna Yusporova gave her husband an exasperated look before turning in her chair to Gaspar. "Ignore them, Gaspar. She's just as lovely as her folks. My guess is she'll be back. But I agree, let's get this conversation started. If you like, I can take notes that we can look back on later."

Gaspar smiled in appreciation at Anna before facing the others around the table. "I appreciate everyone coming this evening. Anna, I think that might be a good idea if we take minutes. We could begin with a roll call."

Anna quickly wrote on her note pad:

- Gaspar Rosso
- Anna and Alex Yusporov
- Alexander Bolitchyn
- Martin and Gayle Shatrov
- Jenny and Nick Kutuz

As she finished, she mentioned that she had seen John Petrov earlier and he planned to come as soon as he finished work for the day.

"Thank you, Anna."

Then, facing those gathered, Gaspar continued, "We all noticed yesterday that the church needed expandable walls, which of course it doesn't have. So, we need to have a good social venue, one at least big enough to hold the entire village for large gatherings. I heard someone mention expanding the church, but that would be a big job. For one thing, we couldn't extend it by very much because of the graveyard. Our other option is to build something like a community hall, but where?"

"Wouldn't that require bringing in heavy equipment? How would we do that—on Joe's barge? What else is required for doing the work?" Martin asked.

"You're right. I believe for equipment we'd just need a backhoe to dig the foundation and yes, I think it could be brought in on Joe's barge. Of course, we'd need to check with Joe to see how much this would cost. Managing this project, though, is no problem because the *what else* is what I learned in Calgary. However, either way it would be a big project and the problem I see is time. If we want everything completed by the New Year's celebration, we need to get started right away. Renovating an existing building will be much harder than just building a new building from scratch."

As everyone at the table began to slowly process this information, they began to nod their heads in assent.

Paul, who was enjoying an early supper with Christella at a nearby table, turned in his chair and said, "I couldn't help but overhear what you were talking about. I like where your conversation is going, so this is another thought. I'm sure I have heard Bob mention that his *roditeli's* home used to be joined to the Kettle so that they could go between their house and the restaurant without going outside. Maybe you could expand that way."

This got everyone buzzing like summer bees and they immediately called Bob to come over.

"Paul just told us your *roditeli's* home used to join with the restaurant. Is this true?"

"Oh yes," Bob confirmed. Walking over to the back wall, he informed them, "When I was young, this wall didn't exist, and you could move easily between the two places."

Gaspar got up and hurried over to where Bob had indicated. A few minutes later, after having a closer look at the wall, he went back to the table. "This just might work! It may necessitate some structural work on those old, sagging walls, but it's doable, I think. I'll need to come and take a closer look at the outside. Mr. Petrov, do you mind if I come by later in the week?"

"Of course not," Bob replied, "But really, you may want to bring Uri in on your conversation. Now that he's a family man, he's planning to give up fishing. He and Anna will take over the restaurant after my grandbabies are a little older."

This bit of news caused another flutter, before Nick commented, "I'm sure Uri will be excited. Just think, an extra room to the Borscht Kettle means more revenue."

Gaspar eagerly began speaking again. "I was telling my *papa* and Mr. Palmer earlier how, in Calgary, we often spent an evening throwing darts. The extra room here would be perfect. We could order food and sit back to enjoy a companionable evening having a game or two."

"Not only darts," Christella offered as she and Paul got up from their table. "I can think of so many ideas on how we could use the extra space. Like how about hosting a women's craft night? Or playing other games, like Monopoly, or chess. We could even have smaller social functions like special birthday parties, or other special occasions like weddings. I agree, the extra room would be so useful."

Paul, before leaving, added, "I can certainly help with the work anytime our shops are closed. I'm also quite sure John Molodtsov and even his son, Peter, will be eager to help too."

"So, Gaspar, how do you like the sound of a wedding venue?" Alexander asked.

"If my mama has anything to say about it, it'll be Mr. Filipov and Mrs. Rosnokova's wedding, no one else's. If we're done talking about the room, I've got a lot of work to do so I'll go. Let's say we get together next week. By then I should have had time to make a closer inspection." And, leaving his glass half full, he got up and left the room.

———

A week later Gaspar whistled while he jauntily made his way down Marine Street, stopping for a few minutes to enjoy the Canada geese as they flew overhead in their familiar V-shape, honking uproariously. He did an almost skip step as he opened the door to the Borscht Kettle and went in.

"Good to see everyone. Tonight, I have news, and an interesting piece of news at that, to share. Anna, maybe you could start with the roll-call again. When you finish, I'll begin."

"For sure," Anna said, glancing at those around the table before she wrote:

- Gaspar Rosso
- Anna and Alex Yusporov
- Martin Shatrov
- Jenny and Nick Kutuz

This task completed, Gaspar called the meeting to order. "I came by on another day when Mr. Petrov could allow me a closer look at *dedushka* and *babushka* Petrov's home. I went inside, and first, I must say there would be a lot of cleaning up. After Mr. Petrov's *mama* passed away, they moved his *papa* to their home, and nothing was done in the house."

"You mean everything was just left in there?" Anna and Jenny asked incredulously.

"Yes, just like *dedushka* had breakfast that morning and left for the day. Minus the dirt, of course." Gaspar remarked.

Bob, having overheard their comments on the state of his *roditeli's* house, came over to their table.

"Olga was so embarrassed when I came home and told her the condition I found the house in when I was showing Gaspar around. I told her she really shouldn't feel bad. After all, at the time my *mama* passed away, so much was going on in our lives. Anyone who has ever lost someone special to them knows how much of a disruption it is.

"Firstly, my *mama* had been poorly for so long and I could just see how her care was causing a strain on Olga and my sister. After her funeral, my sister spent several days sorting through *Mama's* clothes and then disposing of them. My oldest brother, Nikolai, collected our *papa's* clothes and other personal belongings one afternoon. Of course, at the same time we relocated my *papa* to our home. My brothers William and Arnold took *Papa* back several times, so he could choose a few special things he wanted to keep. You know, items that don't mean anything to anyone else but were important to him.

"Another evening, all five of us siblings and our spouses went and selected something we wanted. I think Alex, your *roditeli* and *dedushka* came and kept my *papa* company that evening. After that, the grandchildren also had an opportunity to save a special reminder of their *babushka*. At the end of the week, when my brothers and their wives returned to Kitimat... well, we were just so exhausted. Olga and I were both working —myself from early morning until late at night. Marg and Merle were just as busy as Olga and me. The children were all still at home and became a great excuse. For weeks we would talk about properly cleaning the home place, but one of us would always have a good reason why they couldn't go that night. As fall turned into winter everyone felt even less like going. By the time the spring came, I think it had slipped all our minds. After all, we had already taken out the items we wanted. It stayed like that until the day I was showing Gaspar and we went inside. Then it hit me like a ton of bricks."

"Mrs. Petrov shouldn't worry herself about it. I can just imagine how distraught everyone must have felt. It's totally understandable how easily a detail like cleaning up your *roditeli* home would be overlooked," Anna consoled him.

After a brief pause, Gaspar continued, "After my inspection, after I tell you my observations, you'll probably understand why I recommend we build something new. We'd need to do a lot of work to restore the house and open this wall again. I noticed signs of rot around the kitchen sink and bathroom floors. My suspicion is there is rot or dry rot in the exterior walls. In some rooms there was evidence of rainwater coming through the roof. This water also caused damage to the floors. Of course, the wiring needs to be brought up to code. I consider everyone's safety to be of upmost importance."

"That sounds like a long list of problems. I agree with tearing it all down and rebuilding," Martin replied.

"I'm in agreement also," Alex said. "If you recommend a new building, Gaspar, that is good enough for me."

"I sure concur with you on the importance of safety. From what you've told us, I wouldn't doubt that the foundation is cracking as well. I second the idea of tearing it all down," Nick agreed.

"Yes, that's also a possibility. I didn't really look at the foundation because I already had a long list of concerns that would substantiate the idea of rebuilding," Gaspar admitted.

"Oh my," Anna said sadly, "I do love the old homes in our village."

"We could always consider gutting it, but putting up a false front or façade to give the appearance of the original house."

"Oh, I like that idea," Anna said, clapping her hands gleefully.

"If we use that space to build a new building and join it up to the Borscht Kettle, I think it will give us the space we need.

It'll be a big project, but I'm confident we can do it. I have a couple of buddies in Calgary, Greg and Kevin. They might be willing to come and help us for a few months. As you know, it may take some time to receive an answer to my letter, but there are things we can do in the meantime."

"Like clean out the items left in the house," Anna suggested.

"Yes, I have already spoken to Mr. Petrov, and he has suggested moving everything to Anna and Uri's place."

"All this talk is great, but my concern is what kind of money is this going to take, and where do you think we can get it?" Nick asked hesitantly.

"Well, I may have an answer to your question, Nick. Just leave it with me for a few days, and hopefully next time we meet I'll have something to tell everyone," Gaspar replied, a slow smile forming at the corners of his lips. "My second piece of news is my *papa* received this letter from the Ministry of Transportation."

Dear Mr. Anthony Rosso:

I am pleased to inform you that secondary road development is planned from Highway 16 through Port Essington to Hartley Bay. This has been an ongoing project for the last several years. As you are no doubt aware, we are working through very difficult terrain.

A portion of this road will cover the approximately fifty miles into New Petrograd. The purpose of this road is to link your village to the numerous secondary roads and highways covering beautiful British Columbia.

Please expect crews to arrive in the area shortly, weather permitting, to begin surveying.

Sincerely,

The Honourable Fraser J. MacDonald

They all looked dumbfounded as everyone set down their drinks and stared at Gaspar. Then, as people began digesting the information, a commotion erupted with everyone talking all at once—asking questions, speaking of all the possibilities, both advantages and disadvantages.

Gaspar finally said, "That's all my news. Does anyone else have anything to add, or any questions?"

After a few minutes he continued, "So, let's meet again next Tuesday evening. I also suggest we get together this Saturday to begin cleaning out the house. The sooner we get started the better."

Anna set down her pen and closed her notebook, thus concluding their second meeting.

As they filed out into the misty night, Alex called to Gaspar, "Great job tonight, Manager."

Everyone agreed.

CHAPTER NINE

The Project

The letter about the road caused a huge stir in the village. Whenever folks saw Tony or Gaspar, they hailed them to ask if it was true. Tony took to carrying the letter in his pocket, so he could produce it on request. The people of the village were impressed to see the official government seal. As it was read, everyone seemed to gleefully drink in every word. Tony never tired of reading it, but he chuckled over dinner one night that it was getting very frayed.

Frank and Betty were concerned that they would lose business, as with the new road, places like Kitimat or Prince Rupert were going to become more accessible for shopping. This fear had been hushed by anyone who overheard them express their qualms.

Phil expressed pleasure at the realization that he could take Marg for a lovely drive and dinner. Before he realized one thing. "Well, Marg could drive me, I guess." Because of course he didn't have a vehicle or driver's license yet.

Marg said thoughtfully, "I'm so happy there'll be no more bumping along on bush roads, especially with my old bones."

Tony felt sure Daria would agree.

Marvin and June were thrilled as they admitted driving was something they had missed.

Many of Gaspar's friends now expressed their feelings of jealousy that he had learned to drive while he was living in Calgary. Their envy turned to pleasure when he offered to teach them.

———

As Tony and Gaspar made their way through the village one morning, the first thought on Gaspar's mind was his new truck. Scott had managed to find a 1981 Ford F-250, which he claimed was in mint condition. If there was a second thought, it was elation about all the places he'd be able to drive. There was still a long wait until the road would be constructed, but he was enjoying the anticipation.

As the barge was coasting up to the pier, Ray and Bill stopped work long enough to wave. Once they had secured it, the men began bringing ashore their usual assortment of boxes. Gaspar fidgeted with his jacket zipper, as he not so patiently waited.

Finally, Scott drove the vehicle on to the wharf.

"How's it going, man?" Scott greeted him, as he stepped out of the vehicle and handed the keys to Gaspar.

"Great," Gaspar replied. "I need to give you my cheque for payment of this baby. How about I meet you in John's Kiosk and we can take care of business and have a good chat over a cup of coffee?"

"That works just fine for me. Let me finish up here and I'll be along shortly. I'm sure the other guys will want to come as well. They seemed stoked that we'd see you this morning. Of course, that was an assumption, but it did seem to be almost a guarantee, with us having your vehicle on board."

"See you in a few minutes, then," Gaspar said, as he stood on the running board before climbing inside. Then, leaning out the window while starting the engine, he called to his *papa* where he was showing Joe the letter. Tony quickly folded the letter and put it into his back pocket. He said some final words to Joe and came around to the passenger door.

"I'm meeting the crew in a few minutes at the kiosk, *Papa*. Would you like to come, or should I give you a quick lift home?"

"I made coffee arrangements with Joe also, so I'll go along with you," Tony responded.

As Gaspar and Tony entered the kiosk, the bell over the door chimed, announcing their arrival.

John lifted his head to see who his latest customers were, calling out a pleasant, "Hello, Mr. Rosso and Gaspar."

He then turned back to the two people standing with him at the counter. Gaspar realized with a start that it was John's sister Anna and his brother-in-law Uri, with their new babies.

"Hello, everyone," Gaspar called, and then hurried over to congratulate Anna and Uri, and to get a closer look at the twins. "Sure, haven't seen much of you two lately," Gaspar teased as he came abreast of them.

Tony was on his heels and exclaimed, "How delightful seeing you here. I simply love babies."

When Tony arrived at the counter, Uri handed him Matthew, taking time to swaddle the blanket a little tighter. "It sure is nice to know that, in a few years, we'll have many *dedushkas* to call on for babysitting," Uri teased.

"What do you mean, in a few years? What about now?"

Anna said, as she eyed Tony. Then turning to Gaspar, she added, "Would you like to hold Madeline?"

Reaching out for her, he replied, "I'd love to cuddle her. I was always sorry I had no younger siblings to play with."

"Well, as you know, that wasn't because your *mama* and I didn't want more children." Then, directing his comments to everyone else in the room, Tony said, "Daria had several miscarriages, so we were as pleased as punch when Gaspar arrived. He might not have weighed very much, but he had ten fingers and ten toes and was healthy. He has brought much joy in our lives, and he still does."

"Aw, *Papa*," Gaspar grunted in embarrassment, as he shook his head, sighing loudly.

They all looked at Tony in dismay, before Uri finally broke the silence by saying, "Our family has certainly been keeping us close to the house. For a while we thought Madeline might need more medical attention. Thankfully the district nurse came this morning and helped resolve the problem, but I feel I can empathize a bit with you, Mr. Rosso," Uri said. "Madeline didn't seem to be able to feed, and I've never been so scared. Stormy seas and high winds lashing against my fishing boat weren't nearly as frightening as my wee daughter facing her first challenge of her short life."

"Yes, it was a bit scary for awhile, but she has good Russian blood and she is getting better," Anna told them. "I'm pleased to see you, Gaspar. I guess my *papa* mentioned to you that Uri and I are planning to take over the business when he finally retires."

"He did."

"Anna, I told you before, remember, if our *rhotideli* want to retire before you feel able to work, I am certainly willing to let you do the lighter tasks, like selling chocolate bars and magazines. I can help Uri. The heavier postal work I can still take care of in my off hours, or send Sandy down to help you."

"Thank you, John. I do remember, and both Uri and I appreciate your offer." Anna smiled at her brother.

"Yes, John, your offer is very thoughtful, but I think Anna is best staying at home taking care of our babies for a few months. I don't want her taking on extra work outside of our home. These two bundles keep her very busy and very, very tired."

"Really though, John, I think it is *Mama* that wants to retire the most, not *Papa*. She often says how tired she is at the end of the day. Yesterday I heard her tell Betty Yusperova that perhaps the school jurisdiction could send a substitute if they haven't hired someone to move here permanently. I believe when this school year ends, *mama* will finish her career.

"Madeline and Matthew haven't helped the situation either, because I sense what she really wants most is to be a full-time *babushka*. John if you want to keep your *mama* happy, you and Sandy had better hurry and catch up."

Uri, reaching for Matthew, and at the same time focusing his attention on Gaspar, said, "I really would like a chat but just before you came in Anna was saying it's feeding time. For now, we'd best be going home."

Gaspar smiled his response as he gave Madeline a peck on the top of her head and handed her back to her *mama*. Just then the door opened and in spilled Phil and Joe with the mailbags, and right behind them the rest of the crew.

The kiosk soon came alive with all the chatting between the tables where Tony and Joe sat and the one where Gaspar and the crew were. Finally, Joe called to his staff, exclaiming they had best grab a quick lunch at the Kettle and be off, if they wanted to keep on schedule.

Everyone stood and shoved back their chairs.

"Did you remember to tell him about the gas, Scott?"

"Oh yeah. We filled the tank. You know the adage, if you give a person a new wallet you put a penny in it. Joe suggested that if we were delivering a new truck, why not fill the tank? So we pooled our money and filled it."

"Gee, thanks! A tank should get me quite a few circles around this village."

In reply he got a wave of their hands and a chuckle, as they exited the Kiosk.

As Gaspar and Tony where leaving, Gaspar turned at the door and called back to John that they were planning their first workday on Saturday to clean out his *dedushka's* place.

The trip home was a mere five minutes; just long enough for Tony to relate his and Joe's conversation that many of the hamlets on Joe's route had received similar letters from the ministry.

Daria was eagerly looking out the window and at the sight of them came out to admire Gaspar's vehicle.

"Oooh," she said approvingly, "I do love its shiny red colour and black interior. Son, when are you going to take me for a drive around town?" Then she hustled everyone inside for tomato soup and grilled cheese sandwiches.

CHAPTER TEN
Work Begins

Gaspar groaned when he turned over in bed to hear rain pounding on the roof. A quick check of his alarm clock informed him he needed to get up and face another rainy day. After he had showered and was pulling on his jeans and getting a clean sweater from his dresser drawer, he had cheered up a little. By the time he had finished his breakfast and was pulling on his rain slicker and hood, he was feeling ready for the day.

"At least," Daria offered, "Most of your work will be indoors. June and I are planning on working on our macramé projects today, but—" She smiled. "—I have a sneaking suspicion we'll end up at Bob's *roditeli's* home."

"Marvin and I had the same idea. This village... well, I don't know when it has seen excitement like this." Then, with a wink to Gaspar, Tony added, "We need to get a look at our soon-to-be social room where the dart board can be set up."

Gaspar jumped into his truck and drove away thinking how good it felt to be behind the wheel again. He groaned inwardly, though, when he turned off Marine Street and saw most of the village residents standing under their umbrellas. "Oh well." He smiled to himself. "I might have known that news of this project would spread. Like *Papa* said, I don't know when the village has seen excitement like this."

Getting out of his truck, he hurried across the street to where the townspeople were huddled and, greeting his neighbours with a bright smile, led the way to the old Petrov house. Soon the men were loading the furniture on to Bob's and Frank's trucks to move it all to Anna and Uri's home. Marg and Olga had attempted to wash some of the dishes, but it was soon evident the water pipes had corroded and there was no water. Shrugging, they decided they would have to pack the dishes as they were. Sandy and Jenny were organizing the ladies in wrapping anything breakable in newspaper and putting things in boxes Anna's in-laws had brought from their store.

Betty and Frank had closed the store for the day. "No one's going to be shopping today, anyway, with all this excitement going on."

When Gaspar saw his *papa*, he made his way over to him and asked if Mr. Palmer had come with him.

"Yes, I lost him at the door. I think he went to speak to June in the kitchen."

"Thanks, *Papa*. I'll see if I can catch him there."

Gaspar was just making his way to the kitchen when he saw Marvin leaving, so he called after him. When Marvin stopped and turned with a big grin, Gaspar came closer, and then asked if he could have a word with him, perhaps Sunday or Monday night?

"You sure can," Marvin replied, giving Gaspar a fatherly thump on the back. "I think I can anticipate why you want to see me, and the answer is yes. Come by when it is convenient, and we can work out the details."

"Thank you, I sure appreciate it. It'll probably be tomorrow when I come. Our committee has been meeting Tuesday nights, so I'd like to be able to share the news with them." Then he hurried off to see why Martin and Mr. Filipov were zealously waving him over.

By noon the work crew, dirty and dishevelled, started staggering their visits to the Borscht Kettle, as Bob had extended an invitation to serve everyone a light lunch. By now most of the big pieces of furniture had been moved. Anna, Sandy, and Jenny were suggesting to the other women that they could finish up, but they didn't seem to be listening, because after they had their lunch, everyone returned. Although there were still boxes full of items going to Anna and Uri's, the pile of things now to be thrown out was growing. In the late afternoon, when Gaspar observed how much the pile had expanded, he grabbed Alexander and suggested they start taking things to the dump.

It had taken most of the day when Gaspar, exhausted, finally closed the door and, wiping a hand across his dirty brow, gave a huge thank you to everyone who was still there. Then he raced the raindrops back to where his truck was parked.

————

The following Tuesday, when the committee met, everyone was still pumped up over the amazing day Saturday had been. Gaspar's news that he had visited with Mr. Palmer, who was keen to offer funding for the new building, only kept the temperature in the room soaring.

A chorus of exclamations of "Mr. Palmer!" went up from

everyone, even causing Bob to look up from where he was serving a cup of hot tea to Gayle.

This seemed to jolt Anna into realizing she hadn't taken roll call. Her eyes swiftly moved around the table as her hand did a marathon in writing the names down. She was smiling as she realized everyone was there, even John and Sandy Petrov.

"Uh yes, Mr. Palmer," Gaspar muttered, his face flushing when he realized his mistake in saying the name of their benefactor.

The committee then wasn't satisfied until Gaspar had told the whole story of why the Palmers were happy to provide funding.

"As the village's financial person and notary public, that information sure sets my mind at ease," Nick said. "I suspect Mr. Palmer will soon be creating a new account and transferring some money into it."

"He will," Gaspar agreed. "I just wanted to share the news with everyone first. I expect you'll see him tomorrow or the next day."

When Gaspar was finished telling his story, a smiling Bob, shaking his head incredulously, said, "I can appreciate they won't want to be recognized but, in my mind, I'll think of this new addition as the Palmer room."

Everyone heartily agreed.

Gaspar then went onto say that this meant he'd be able to visit the general store to place an order for the lumber and other supplies that would be needed.

"The third item on my agenda is this Saturday. I'd like to start tearing down the old house. However, my advice is, don't let anyone else know of our plans. I think it'll be much safer if there are just a few of us."

There were comments from some of the women on

whether they could accompany their husbands, but Gaspar was adamant that he only wanted the men. Although a few protests went up, he just ignored them.

Finally, looking briefly at Anna, he said with a sympathetic smile, "You would only cry."

Anna had to agree she would. Just thinking about it, she admitted, she had started getting teary.

Looking around the table at their pouting faces, Gaspar hesitantly said, "You know, I just had a thought. If you ladies would make us a few signs with words like *Caution, Danger*, and *Keep Back*, it would be very helpful. We can place them around the job site to help keep it safe. That way everyone in the village will be safe as well. Will you see if Mr. Yusperov has anything in his store that may be waterproof? Otherwise, you can just use large sheets of paper and tell him to charge the cost to the project."

Gaspar smiled when he was rewarded with several nodding heads and cheerful faces. Sandy said she could pick up the supplies and suggested they gather at her and John's place to make them.

"Let's say we start just after lunch on Saturday. Then we should have the signs ready just before dusk."

"Perfect," Gasper approved.

As the meeting concluded and everyone was pushing their chairs back and putting on their coats, Gaspar, his coat partially zipped, stopped and apologized. "Oh, and I almost forgot. I have one more item. My *papa* concurs that we've made the right decision to start with a new building."

Afterwards, they traipsed out in small groups, still commenting on what a positive meeting it had been. Then they stepped outside to battle a freezing wind that held whispers of snow in it.

On Saturday Alex, Alexander, Martin, and Nick were able to come. The men were pleased that the day was dry, although as some noted, the temperature seemed to have dropped another few degrees.

Gaspar started by commenting that he was eager to get the old house torn down before the snow began to fall.

"Today we'll start with the roof. Then, if there is time before it gets dark, the walls. The inner sections of the house will come last," he directed.

As many of the village folk went about their Saturday activities, they stopped for a few minutes to watch, often shaking their heads as if in disbelief. Then they would continue on their way.

Halfway through the day, the men made their way to the Borscht Kettle for their noon meal. Most importantly though, for many of the men it was a reprieve from the cold cloak they had worn all morning. As they ate their meal of *rassolnik* soup, Gaspar admitted that what he liked best about it was the pickles, only to be told by Alex that the beef and barley would give him more nutrition.

Bob approached them as the ate their hearty meal of soup and made the generous offer to buy everyone steel-toed boots. "Just go to see Frank and place an order for your boot size. Frank is aware that I'll be covering the cost."

A shocked look came on everyone's face as slowly it registered what Bob had just offered. Then everyone was calling out *thank you*. Gaspar's thank you was the loudest, not because he needed a new pair of boots, but because he appreciated that they would make everyone safer while working.

The men returned to work for the afternoon, warmed by

Bob's offer. By dusk they had successfully managed to dismantle the roof. Alexander again had tirelessly assisted Gaspar in moving the debris to the garbage dump. Before they left for home, they braced the walls, making sure everything at the job site was secure.

Nick looked up and alerted everyone else as the men observed several of their wives coming towards them, carrying the signs.

Sandy called out as they came within ear shot, "Mr. Yusperov didn't have anything waterproof, but he did have this poster paper he had ordered for Olga at the schoolhouse. He only had it in purple, but we told him we thought it would work just fine."

"It will, won't it, Gaspar?" Martin asked, as the reached to take them from the ladies' hands.

"Yes. Thank you so much for doing them. It really is an enormous help."

————

Gaspar's opening comments the following Tuesday were that it was a month after Thanksgiving. His statement left the unspoken thought that they were that much closer to the end of the year, and their goal to have everything finished. His next words, though, lifted everyone's spirits. He had heard from his friends. They would be arriving the following week and, conveniently, so would all the building supplies.

"Our work will speed up then, as Greg and Kevin can devote every day to working on the job. My *roditeli* are looking forward to their staying with us. Arriving on the barge Thursday will mean they'll be here for fish and chips night, when I hope everyone can introduce themselves. I plan to put them to work next Saturday. It's been suggested that they also remove the old community cold cellar, which will allow for some extra space. This Saturday I'm hoping we have another great turnout to remove the exterior walls. Once we begin removing them, for safety reasons, I believe we must stay until the job is finished."

Anna, who was preoccupied with taking the minutes, lifted her head and with a brief look at her husband, suggested that everyone come to their place Thursday evening. "Fish and chips nights are so busy, so hectic, that I am sure we can get a better visit this way."

Alex was about to speak, when Alexander cut him off. "Everyone?"

"Yes," Alex said. Then starting with Alexander and perusing everyone around the table, he went on, "My wife and I would be thrilled to host you all, and your friends, Gaspar."

Jenny and Sandy were beginning to ask Anna what she would like them to bring, but Nick brought the meeting back on topic. "Perhaps we could ask your *papa* and Mr. Palmer to help us this Saturday."

A vote around the table indicated everyone was in favour of this suggestion. Gaspar concluded another week's meeting by saying, "I will ask them."

———

Gaspar was sure the temperature had dropped even lower, but nothing could chill his mood. He believed they would reach a milestone this weekend. His *papa* and Marvin had happily accepted the invitation to help and they were following him now, in *Papa's* truck. Gaspar had informed them earlier that all the male members of the committee were expected to show up today. Sure enough, when he drove in sight of the house, all the men were waiting. In addition, John Molodostov and his son, Peter, were also there. As he made his way towards them, he smiled in amusement as Peter was hopping from one foot to the other. Whether from excitement or the cold, Gaspar couldn't be sure; some of the men were also blowing into their cupped hands. Gaspar took note, with pleasure, that the men were now wearing their new boots. With the temperature dropping, he knew things around the job site would soon become slippery.

The old house was being dismantled quickly with the efforts of all these men. They worked hard, taking only the briefest of breaks all day. Board by board was taken down... and it was with a great cheer from everyone that the last of the outside walls were removed and carted away.

CHAPTER ELEVEN

Kevin and Greg Arrive

A light snow was falling on Thursday morning when Gaspar drove to the pier to meet Joe's barge and, most important, his buddies. Kevin and Greg were all smiles, waving as the barge came in to dock.

"Hello, you two," Gaspar called. "Your first job is to load the lumber and the other supplies onto my truck."

"Nothing like breaking us in easy," Kevin hollered back.

"Joe's been treating us like we're on a luxury cruise, letting us lie around and laze for the last six days. How about some sightseeing first?"

"Don't believe a word they say," Joe called as he and Scott started moving boxes off the barge. "It seems to me that they never stopped finding things to do."

When they finally came ashore, Gaspar gave them both a welcoming thump on the back before saying seriously, "After we load and unload the lumber, I'll let you have the rest of the day off to sightsee around the village. The tour will start with me introducing you to my *roditeli* and ends with a Russian meal tonight at the home of my good friends, Alex and Anna."

There were so many supplies that the men quickly realized it was going to take more than one trip to move it using the pickup. When they arrived with the first truckload, Gaspar let out an exclamation of surprise. "There is my *papa* setting down some planks for us to stack this lumber on.

"Thanks, *Papa*, this is a huge help. Those boards will keep the supplies off the wet ground." By now it was lightly covered in snow. Then, remembering his manners, Gaspar introduced Greg and Kevin.

"Welcome, welcome," Tony said while shaking Kevin's hand. "We are quite looking forward to your visit. Gaspar, I also brought some tarps to cover the lumber. We need to keep the supplies as dry as possible."

"Pleased to meet you, Mr. Rosso," Kevin said. "I'm glad to have an opportunity to visit New Petrograd. Gaspar told us a lot about it when he lived with us. Although I think I'll need to come in the summer to go fishing."

"Well if you'd like to come for a couple of weeks' fishing, I'll fill in for Gaspar, so he can have a holiday as well. There are certainly some great fishing spots nearby."

Gaspar looked at his father with a huge smile and nodded in appreciation.

"That sounds like a great idea. I think I'll plan on that, too," Greg said as he shook Tony's hand.

When Gaspar explained that they needed to make several trips to bring the lumber up from the pier, Tony offered to go home for his truck to help hurry the process. When he returned, Tony said, "You may want to take a break for lunch this load. Your *mama* has it ready and waiting."

"Good idea," Gaspar replied. "I know I'm hungry enough to eat a bear, and I think I've heard some other stomachs rumble too." Looking at Kevin and Greg with a twinkle in his eye, he said, "We'll stop to pick up their luggage from John's, where we left it earlier. This won't take us long, so you can tell *Mama* we're on our way."

Daria must have been listening for his vehicle, because she was standing at the door a little breathless, as if she had just run from the kitchen. Gaspar lazily draped his arm about his *mama's* shoulder while introducing his friends to her. Then he asked, "What's to eat?"

"Nice to meet you, Mrs. Rosso," Kevin and Greg said in unison while giving Gaspar a dirty look. He laughingly shrugged it off and led the way down the hall to the kitchen.

"It looked so cold this morning that I decided to make a chili recipe June gave me," she said, as she began to lift a huge pot off the stove. Tony hurried to take it from her and set it on the table.

"Thank you dear. Now Gaspar, can you get the green salad from the fridge and serve everyone a drink? I'll take this garlic bread out of the oven and slice it. Then we should be ready to eat."

It was a pleasant meal, with Kevin and Greg telling about their trip there or asking questions about the village. Suddenly Gaspar noticed the time and, jumping up from the table, exclaimed, "We'd better get a move on! *Papa*, do you mind helping us move the lumber until we're finished? I promised Kevin and Greg a sightseeing tour and then we're going to have supper at Alex and Anna's."

"I reckon the sightseeing tour will take no more than a half hour, but you're right, the building materials will take longer," Tony commented as he also got up from the table.

"Thank you, Mrs. Rosso," Kevin said.

"Sorry to leave you with all these dishes," Greg said, before he raced down the hall after the others.

"Just enjoy your afternoon," Daria called after them.

When they went outside, everyone was pleased to see it had stopped snowing, leaving only a light dusting of white sparkling on everything. It was late afternoon and already getting dusky when they finished getting the rest of the supplies moved and secured under the tarp. Gaspar took a quick drive past the old church, pointing out the founding fathers' plaque, before stopping by the Borscht Kettle for warm drinks. All they ordered were glasses of *mors* and a *medovukha*, which Gaspar explained were not much more than fruit drinks.

Around six o'clock they made their way to Alex and Anna's house. As they walked to the door Gaspar grimaced, realizing he had used his muscles differently today than he had recently. They were letting him know. He was careful not to wince or his friends would be sure to notice, and if they did, they'd tease him mercilessly. Alex already had the door open, ushering them in. Gaspar noticed with satisfaction that everyone was already there, and he quickly introduced Greg and Kevin. Anna had prepared beef stroganoff, *knish*, and a green salad, with *kissel* to finish.

"This small pie sure is good. What is it?" Greg asked, holding up a forkful of *knish*.

"It's called potato *knish*," Anna explained. "The pastry is filled with potatoes, sauerkraut, and onions."

Kevin said, "I thought the same, Greg. I'm enjoying my first taste of Russian food, that's for sure."

"Thank you," Anna said, smiling at them both.

It was a jovial evening and in no time, Gaspar could see Kevin and Greg relaxing and fitting in. Of course, Alexander was true to form, and kept everyone laughing. Kevin and Greg again shared stories of their trip on the barge and spoke of their respect for Joe and his crew.

"What a life," Kevin said. "Working a job that means being on the ocean most of the time."

"It's a hard life," Uri replied, while rocking one of the twins. "You're constantly away from your family. Now that I am a family man, I have my fishing boat up for sale. Although no one has made me an offer yet."

"I know, I know," Kevin said. "But for a single guy like me—I think I'd love to do it for a few years. Joe said he'd give me a call if he heard of anyone needing a deckhand. I'd like to work with Joe, but he already has a great crew. I can't wish for any one of them to quit."

"Yeah, that would be neat," Gaspar commented "I'd get to see you once a week."

"I don't agree with you, Gaspar; it wouldn't be neat," Greg responded. "With first you, and now this guy, threatening to leave, I'd have no roommates left."

And a collective *awwww* was heard around the room, as several sighed in mock sympathy.

The highlight of the evening was when Anna gave a brief account of the founding fathers' journey to New Petrograd. She focused especially on the home they were now dismantling, which was once the happy home of Nikolai and Margarita Petrov. They had raised five children there, but only Bob Petrov and Marg Rosnokova had stayed in the village.

"Mr. Petrov and his wife, Olga, own the Borscht Kettle, which I'm sure Gaspar will take you to. Marg Rosnokova was a housewife, and now that she's a widow, she's dating the lighthouse keeper, Mr. Filipov. Mr. Petrov has informed me his three brothers moved to Kitimat to work for Alcan. They rarely come home."

"Perhaps with the new road going through, they'll be able to come here more often," her husband said.

"That's a nice thought," Anna agreed.

Gaspar mentioned that he had already taken his friends to the Kettle for a drink prior to coming there tonight. "It really didn't matter what we ordered, but I did want to introduce them to Mr. Petrov."

"Oh good." Anna said." Then she added, tongue in cheek, "It's good that you're showing them all the highlights, Gaspar."

"Well, he didn't just take us there, he also drove us past the founding fathers' plaque that you mentioned," Greg said.

When Gaspar saw both Kevin and Greg holding back yawns, he decided it was time to go home. Admittedly, he was stifling a yawn as well.

The following morning, Gaspar went to do some renovations at a few homes. He left Kevin and Greg with his *roditeli* enjoying the fire his *papa* had built in the fireplace.

"How about if we meet you at the Borscht Kettle tonight?" his *mama* asked him as he left for his workday.

"That should work," he agreed. "Whoever arrives first can hold a table for five." Then, addressing Kevin and Greg, he said, "You're in for another treat tonight—a local tradition."

As he drove off, Gaspar was feeling most appreciative of Anna's meeting notes, which he had left with Kevin and Greg, so they could read them.

CHAPTER TWELVE

Skeleton in Cold Storage

Gaspar stirred in his sleep and rolled over, trying to get comfortable again in a different position. Then realization struck him as he wrinkled his nose. He smelled bacon cooking. *Mama*, or somebody else, was in the kitchen. He rolled the other way, so he could get a quick glance at his clock. It read 6:30.

Coming downstairs, he could hear his buddies talking to his *mama*. From what conversation he could make out, they were obviously helping her in the kitchen. He felt a slight groan rise inside him as he realized he was the last one up.

"Well, good morning, sleepyhead," Greg said as he stepped into the kitchen.

"Hey, boss, are you taking liberties with the territory?" Kevin jokingly asked him.

"That's right," Gaspar informed them. "Being late is just proof I am the boss. Therefore, I will take advantage of my prerogatives."

"I don't know, Greg, did we sign a contract for this job?"

"Nope. I propose we catch the next barge out of here. Mrs. Rosso, can we stay until Thursday, when Joe comes back?"

"The only thing you two need to worry about next Thursday and the barge is whether a backhoe will come with it," Gaspar told them. "Then you can start digging the foundation. Between now and then, your assigned task is to dismantle the required buildings."

Daria was enjoying the playful banter going on between her son and his chums while she prepared their breakfast. Finally, she informed them, "Grab a seat, breakfast is ready."

As Daria pulled back a chair to sit at the table, Gaspar looked around the kitchen. "Where's *Papa*?"

"I'm right here," Tony's muffled voice answered from his workshop.

A few minutes later he joined them in the kitchen, carrying a sledgehammer. Obviously, he planned to accept Gaspar's invitation to help his friends today.

"Does everyone have one of these?" Tony inquired, as he held up the crowbar. "I have a few more in my workshop, if you don't."

"We do," Kevin answered, as he took another spoonful of *guriev* porridge. "We tried to anticipate the tools we might need and brought them with us."

"Great," Tony said, as he joined them at the table. "Good breakfast, dear," he remarked, after he had eaten a few spoonsful of porridge.

"Thank you, darling," Daria replied as she got up to bring more toast. "Does anyone need anything while I'm up? More coffee, perhaps?"

A few shakes of their heads were the only answer she received.

"I agree, *Papa*. This sure hits the spot."

"*Mama*, you're spoiling us. You must have gotten up very early to prepare this," Gaspar noted, as he took his last spoonful.

"When you're responsible for feeding such an important work crew, you need to start their day right. Really, though, it wasn't too much trouble. The porridge is made from semolina and milk, with nuts, milk skins, and dried fruits. Preparing the milk skins is what takes the longest."

When breakfast was over, the men loaded all the tools they anticipated needing for the day into Gaspar's truck. Then they divided into groups, Kevin and Gaspar driving and Tony and Greg walking.

As they made their way to the village centre, Tony said, "Gaspar's been driving his truck nearly every day since he got it. I understand this morning why he feels he needs it to bring your tools. Then of course it does come in handy for taking things to the dump. However, I do think he should be conserving gas. We only get one large barrel delivered weekly."

"I imagine that's a challenge for him," Greg replied. "There's a gas station on the corner of almost every major intersection in Calgary."

Tony remarked in surprise, "Is that so? I can't even picture that." By now they were approaching the job site. Then he looked down the street as if he was trying to imagine it.

"What are you looking so quizzical about?" Gaspar asked, turning to look down the street, too.

"I am visualizing a gas station on every street corner. I was just expressing my concerns to Greg that you're using your truck every day. We may need to ask Joe to deliver a separate barrel of gas just for you. That'll leave Bob, Frank and me, and occasionally Marg, to share the other barrel."

"Enough talk," Gaspar playfully responded, grinning at

him. "There is no need to worry, *Papa*. I'm still using the tank that Joe and his crew bought me."

Then he started sharing his thoughts on what work he'd like to see accomplished that day. As he finished speaking, he turned to see some of the village men walking towards them.

"It's sure great that you came today to help. I'm thinking there are four men here with experience and four without. Why don't the men without skills each partner with one who does. That way as we remove walls, there is a man to assist pulling it away and leaving it for trash."

Soon in different areas of the house the men had gone to work. Often it almost seemed the sledgehammers pounded in time with each other. A great pile of rubbish was forming on the ground waiting to be taken to the dump.

"Maybe we should be saving some of this wood to have a big bonfire on the beach next summer," Martin suggested.

"I don't know," Tony replied. "It may not dry out. Then all you'll have is a lot of smoke."

"I agree with you Martin," said John Molodtsov. "It may well be worth taking some of it to the beach and try. After all these years, it's bone dry. I'm thinking of those hot dogs Mr. Palmer served the kids at their *zakuski* last summer. He told me later they are very popular for roasting on an open fire."

"Yes, I remember overhearing him tell you. He also said they liked to roast marshmallows," Tony added.

"That sounds cool," Paul remarked.

Gaspar stood up from where he was crouched in a corner and arched his back. "All this talk of food is making me hungrier by the minute. Let's break for lunch." So, everyone made their way around the corner to the Borscht Kettle.

A half hour later the men started work again and focused

their efforts for a few more hours. Gaspar called it quits in midafternoon.

"What, this soon?" Nick said. "I thought we'd work until it gets dusky."

"I'd like enough light to show my buddies where the dump is," Gaspar said. "We've got a good-sized pile ready to go. On Monday they'll be on their own."

"Maybe show each of them separately so one remains here?" Tony offered. "We'll keep working until we can't see so well. Hopefully we'll finish taking down the remaining walls by then. Then on Monday, the boys will be able to start removing the flooring and the cold storage shed."

"That sounds great, *Papa*."

Later, as they drove home for supper, Gaspar remarked, "I sure hope I've thought of everything for next week."

"I think so," Greg said. "I'm sure if there's a question, we can put our heads together and easily sort it out."

"I agree, Greg. Gaspar, you've sure been a big help bringing us up to speed."

"As you know, I had many doubts about moving home. I sure am glad I made the choice to do so. It just seems right, and every day the feeling just gets stronger, if that makes any sense. I enjoyed my years in Calgary and getting my construction experience, though."

"And for knowing us," Greg laughed. "If anyone is interested in my opinion, I think Barbara was a fool not to say yes when you asked her."

"Yup, I have to agree with you again," Kevin said. "This seems to be a great village. It's full of kind, friendly people. I'm beginning to think even I could live here and be very content."

Sunday somehow disappeared in a fog, or maybe it should be said a mist, as it rained all day. One good thing was that the rain took care of the light snow that had fallen on Thursday. After church, the household spent the dreary hours of the afternoon playing a very stimulating game of Monopoly. Amongst much friendly jeering and laughter, in the end Kevin narrowly emerged the winner.

On Monday morning, as they drove to the job site, Gaspar, referring to the comments his *Papa* had made to Greg on Saturday, said, "You can't be hauling things off to the dump on foot. If I need to order an extra barrel of gas to be brought here, so be it." Then he happily handed over his truck keys to his friends.

Gaspar even whistled happily as he made his way to Martin and Gayle's home to look at a leaky faucet. For one thing, the day was dry. Although the rainy days were upon them, he could only hope it would stay dry for a bit longer and that the temperature wouldn't drop too low. It needed to be dry for long enough to dig the foundation and pour the cement. Perhaps they could even get it framed in, although he knew this was really pushing their luck.

He arrived home in the early evening to learn his *mama* had invited Mr. and Mrs. Palmer for dinner. "I thought it would be nice to have them over, so they can meet our guests."

This news pleased him. As he made his way into his room to clean up, he wondered about their daughter. He'd been so busy lately that he realized he had only occasionally thought about her. Later, when he went into the living room, the Palmers had arrived. Everyone was there. That is, everyone but Kevin and Greg.

"They seemed pretty sure yesterday that they could handle the work. Maybe they ran into some trouble. I think I'd better go see. After all, it is their first day on their own."

Gaspar was just putting his jacket on when the front door opened, and in walked Kevin and Greg.

"I'm glad you made it home," Gaspar said. "Did you run into a bit of trouble?" When he turned from hanging up his jacket, he caught a look at their faces and exclaimed, "What's wrong with you guys? You look like you've seen a ghost!"

"No," Greg responded, "just a human skeleton." He sank into the first empty chair.

"What are you sputtering about?" Gaspar asked in disbelief.

But the cat seemed to have taken control of their tongues as they stammered out half finished sentences.

"It was awful—"

"I think it was a woman. Least it seemed to be women's clothing in the box. I don't know how long she's been buried, but I think a long time."

"After I took the first glance, I couldn't even look anymore—"

"Oh my," Daria said as she bustled over. "You poor boys. What a fright! Here, both of you, come sit on the couch. No wonder you're so rattled."

Eventually Daria and June calmed them down with soothing words—enough, that is, that they managed to spill the details out. When a strong aroma came floating from the direction of the kitchen, Daria leaped up from where she was kneeling in front of the boys and dashed out. A few minutes later a long, low screech could be heard. "My supper is ruined. What are we going to do?"

Tony raced into the kitchen. Indeed, he could see the charred remains of something unidentifiable dumped in the sink. "Don't worry, dear. We have two options—go to the

Borscht Kettle for dinner, or Bob has started making take-out meals. Maybe we could go there and pick something up."

June, who was following right behind Tony, put her arm around her friend and said, "What a night! Your husband is right. It was much more important to console the boys. Worst case scenario, I could run home and get leftovers."

"*Mama*, how about if I go and get the meals?" Gaspar suggested, as he came into the kitchen.

"I'll go with you," Tony offered. "I think Bob should be informed of this skeleton right away. He may possibly want to move it somewhere this evening. I can help him. Goodness me, I don't know where, though. The church?"

"Good thinking," Marvin said as he grabbed his jacket. "I'll go with you."

"In that case, I'd rather stay home with my friends, *Papa*, if you don't mind picking something up for supper before you come home."

"We can sure do that," Tony said, and the door closed behind them.

An unsettling silence filled the living room. Nobody seemed to know what to do next. No one felt like idle conversation after such a shocking discovery. Even the slightest sound caused everyone to jump.

June finally said, "I've been thinking. Maybe we should talk to Shelley. She might be able to advise us about what should happen next."

At Shelley's name, Gaspar jerked his head up. Then he quietly replied, "That's a really good idea because I sure don't know what to do. Do you mind if I contact her?"

"Of course not. I'm sure you could use Phil's wireless."

———

"Are you insane, Shelley, or just plain crazy?" Gordy said over the phone. "Don't bother answering me, I can answer myself. What I am going to do is phone Lyle and tell him."

"Really!" Shelley snapped. "I only phoned you because I need a ride to the airport. Maybe I'll take a taxi. At least a taxi driver won't hassle me."

Shelley had managed to put a few items in her suitcase when the phone rang again. This time she was greeted by Lyle's deep voice. He barely said hello before starting in on her.

"Shel, what's this Gordy tells me? You're going back to New Petrograd because some guy named Gaspar phoned and said they found a skeleton? And he thinks he needs your help? I agree with Gordy, you must be nuts. Who is this Gaspar?"

"Mom and Dad's neighbour's son."

"Whatever. I'll be over later tonight to talk some sense into you. You always were harebrained, living more in the clouds and fantasizing about your latest scheme."

"I am not! How do you think I manage to do my job, Lyle? All I phoned Gordy for was to ask if he could take me to the airport on Saturday. I didn't take a two-month leave of absence to be listening to the two of you rant. I need to get busy packing."

She was hanging up when she heard Lyle screeching through the phone, "Two months?"

By now she felt unsettled so, on a whim, she decided to grab her purse and head to the Oakridge Mall. She needed to cool down a little. Besides, she planned on purchasing some things she knew her mother would appreciate. But when she opened the door, she saw both of her brothers coming down the apartment building's corridor and she took note of the set expressions on their faces.

"You can't escape this time," Lyle began. "First, maybe you can tell us who this Gaspar is, other than somebody's son, who has just found a skeleton in his closet."

"Very funny. The skeleton was found in a cold storage space. I guess in the past it was used by the whole community, so goodness knows who put the body there. Or, for that matter, who they were. Another question is, did anyone report her missing? These people need help, they need direction. They have no idea how to manage the situation. I'm more than happy to help them out. By the way, it was Mom's suggestion that they call me."

Then she turned and stomped back into her apartment. With her brothers, there was no option but to accept defeat and sit and listen. Whether she paid attention to them or not was her choice.

———

Tuesday night at the meeting, as she was writing down the names, Anna noticed again that everyone was in attendance. This always gave her a thrill.

Gaspar cleared his throat and wearily began, "I believe everyone was there at Alex and Anna's on Thursday evening. So, everyone has met Kevin and Greg already. I'd like to add what an enjoyable evening the other night was. On Friday I had them read the minutes from our previous meetings. They were grateful for these notes to help them understand what work has already been done. Kevin and Greg have managed to finish taking the remainder of the house down. I'm very pleased with how much work they've managed to do in just a few days.

"This Thursday, when Joe comes, he'll be delivering a backhoe. This will allow us to begin digging the foundation. My biggest fear is that if it gets much colder, we'll need a steamer truck to thaw the permafrost. Firstly, my concern would be that the truck would be much too heavy to come by barge. Secondly, I'm concerned that the cost might challenge the budget that's been worked out with Nick and Mr. Palmer."

Kevin spoke up. "I don't think a steamer will be necessary. My observation has been that we could make do with a frost bucket."

"What is a frost bucket?" Martin asked.

"It's a smaller bucket with sharper teeth that you put on the backhoe to allow it to dig through ice. Regular buckets are just flat and don't have any teeth. Like Gaspar says, hopefully we won't need to do anything that extreme."

"Yes," Greg added. "The best part is, we would just require a small rubber tire backhoe. Without a basement, we only need to dig down four feet for the foundation."

As Nick looked from one to the other, a smile formed on his face. "Thanks for your detailed answer." Then he visibly relaxed back in his chair.

"Incidentally, I seem to recall when someone needed a new house, they'd hire a company from Prince Rupert. They brought all their own men and equipment. It certainly is much nicer to have friends at our disposal."

"Your right, Gaspar," Anna agreed. "When we built our house it was the company from Rupert. What was their name? I think it was something like Splendid Ocean View Homes. They weren't nearly as personable as Kevin and Greg are."

"We had them build our house also. I agree, Anna, we couldn't complain about their work, but they weren't very friendly," Martin added.

Even as she spoke the word *personable* a slight frown flashed across Anna's usually serene face. Kevin and Greg certainly didn't seem to have the same vim and vigor that they'd had the other night. In fact, she thought they seemed quite subdued. She had heard the rumours that had been floating around the village, about their finding a skeleton. They had even talked about it the other night when Alex's *roditeli* and *dedushka* had visited. During the conversation she had noticed *dedushka* becoming quite fidgety. Alex had noticed too and they had even talked about it later.

Gaspar continued, "After digging the foundation, the next step is pouring the cement. We all need to keep our fingers crossed that the weather continues to hold during this process. Then we can begin framing the new building. Greg has a Master Electrician's ticket and a Red Seal, so he can handle any electrical work. We'll need to hire a plumber, though, if we want to put in a washroom. It would finish things off better in the new area if we did this. I can do some plumbing, but not enough. We're maybe three weeks away from completing everything if we can keep this same pace. However, we do still have a lot of work. It will be much appreciated anytime any of you men can help." A glimmer of a smile appeared on Gasper's face when he finished speaking. "This is all I have for tonight's agenda. I am very tired. I am quite certain my buddies are also. Maybe we should just finish here and have an early night." Then abruptly, he closed the meeting.

"What about the human skeleton I've heard rumours of?" Alexander shouted.

"Yes, tell us what you know about the skeleton," several voices said in agreement.

"I know nothing about the skeleton other than Mr. Petrov and my *papa* moved the crude coffin it was buried in. Where they moved it, I do not know. We'll need to discuss this whole situation with the authorities, but I believe at this time nothing has been arranged."

Then he stood and zipped up his jacket, as his buddies pushed back their chairs. As he lifted his head, he couldn't help but notice a strange look pass between Anna and Alex. He wondered why, and whether he had said something to upset them, but he didn't take the time to ask.

The three chums quietly walked home with none of their usual banter. And very little conversation. Each seemed lost in his own thoughts.

Gaspar's thoughts were, admittedly, about a certain someone with long blonde hair. She had seemed very happy to receive his call the other evening, regardless of the reason. Most important, she had agreed to come.

CHAPTER THIRTEEN

Disruption in New Petrograd

For the first time in its history on an ordinary workday, Bob closed the Borscht Kettle so that they could hold a meeting in privacy. Shelley had told him she wanted to brief everyone on what they could expect to happen. She also said the sooner the better, and he had heartily agreed.

The invitation had been given to Gaspar, his *roditeli*, his friends, and the Palmers. Bob had automatically started pouring alcoholic drinks like beer and *tarasun*, believing everyone would want something stronger than coffee or tea.

Shelley began by saying she was glad everyone had accepted Bob's invitation. She then continued with the rest of the information she wished to share. Before she'd left Vancouver, she had put in a request for an RCMP officer to come to New Petrograd. It was confirmed that Sergeant Freedmont would be arriving tomorrow. Coming with him would be a Dr. Gerald Brown, who was the regional coroner. They would fly in from the closest detachment at Prince Rupert.

"Normally an autopsy is performed, but due to the remains being a skeleton, there will only be an examination. I don't know if it can be done in Prince Rupert or if it would need to be flown to Vancouver. I do know they'll need to take the casket with the remains back to their headquarters. The process, which consists of several segments, will begin here."

"What all needs to be done?" Gaspar asked.

"It really depends on their findings," she told him. "The role of the law enforcement officer is to determine if there has been a crime. Was there a suicide, an accident, or worst of all, a murder? They'll consider it a crime scene, and secure the cellar with yellow tape. I'm going check with the sergeant to see if he feels he needs to do this. After all, this isn't a recent crime, if it ever was.

"The coroner, on the other hand, wants to know the cause of death. He'll ask, are there any visible signs of trauma to the body? Once this has been determined the process of identifying them can start. This procedure would normally begin by analyzing fingerprints, dental records, shoe prints, et cetera. In this case, however, not all avenues will be available to the authorities. Therefore, our casualty's clothing will become an important clue, especially the era they came from. It may even be necessary to bring in a forensic anthropologist who, using the skull, could reconstruct the face. With these details, you can perhaps get a picture of the enormous task of identifying not only the cause of death, but the identity of the person."

Looking around the room, Bob was aware of how Shelley's presence and message had seemed to calm everyone. He wasn't foolish enough to think it was the alcohol.

"I'm sorry, because I feel I can't offer you much comfort. I can't even estimate the time this all may take. Until we receive word from the RCMP or we get the corner's report, you will just have to wait as patiently as you can," she concluded.

Bob shook his head, before exclaiming he had never liked

it when his *roditeli* asked him to go and get the root vegetables or mushrooms. "The cellar always seemed creepy. Makes me wonder if I had a sixth sense about the place."

Daria nodded. "I agree, I used to complain to my *mama* that it smelled down there. She would just say it was only the musky earth scent I was smelling and to just do what she asked, and hurry. I would go, but I kept my nose plugged the whole time."

"It is interesting to hear that in your youth you didn't feel comfortable there. Children are often more perceptive than adults. In my work we see it all the time." Shelley smiled. "If there are no more questions or comments, I think that is about all we can do today."

"Well, Greg, if that's it for today, let's get back to work. I can handle this whole situation better when I keep my mind busy." Then with a slight grin Gaspar added, "I have a sixth sense that this good weather won't last."

June and Daria looked at each other as if they knew each other's thoughts. As the door closed behind them, Daria muttered, "You just saw the first flicker of the man who arrived at my home last week."

CHAPTER FOURTEEN
Official Visitors

The sergeant had barely set foot on the wharf when Gaspar and Shelley rushed up to him. Gaspar said, "I'm so glad to see you sir, I mean sirs. This village has been in upheaval ever since last Monday. We've never had anything like this happen before."

"Well, that is what Dr. Brown and I are here to do, to try to resolve the situation, Mr.... uh..."

"Gaspar Rosso, sir. Mr. Petrov is at his place and asked us to meet the seaplane. He operates the Borscht Kettle, our local restaurant, but he felt that meeting at his home would be more appropriate."

"Yes, it is certainly our intent to solve this as quickly as we can," Dr. Brown exclaimed.

The sergeant then turned to face Shelley. "You must be Officer Palmer of the Vancouver P.D.?"

"Yes, I am, Sergeant Freedmont. Welcome to both you and Dr. Brown. I phoned to arrange your visits before I left Vancouver. My parents retired here last summer. The village folk didn't know where to begin when this skeleton was discovered. So, my mother suggested they contact me. I was pleased to take a leave of absence and come to help. I've already explained to some of the residents the process that I believe will take place. I've also let them know that it could be a long time. I know this hasn't been much comfort to them, but at least it gives them some idea of what to expect."

As they made their way to Bob and Olga's home, Sergeant Freedmont said, "Good, I'm glad you came and have also been enlightening everyone as to the process. I think I remember you saying that you were asking for a couple of months' leave from the department. That's a good estimate, although I do hope we can have an answer before then."

"I am sure I can ask for more if I need to."

Bob was waiting at the door when they arrived and shook the men's hands warmly in greeting. "Pleased to meet you both. Do come inside. I'm considered the acting sheriff here, but for most of my years there has been no need for my services."

Not, he thought to himself, until this year.

Both Gaspar and Shelley were pleased to find Olga waiting in the kitchen. When she felt everyone was comfortably seated, Olga then scuttled about, setting cookies on the table and offering to get everyone a drink.

"Take a cookie," Bob invited, as he passed them to Dr. Brown.

"Appreciate it," Dr. Brown replied as he took one, and passed the plate on to Shelley.

Sergeant Freedmont took a bite of his cookie and, casually turning it around in his fingers, inquired, "Where was the skeleton found, and by whom?"

"It was found in what used to be a communal cold storage space," Gaspar explained. "It hasn't been used for years. We tore down an old house and still wanted some extra room, so we were tearing down the cold storage space as well. You see, our final project is to create more space that we can access from the Borscht Kettle. Using the cold storage area will increase the space by a few more feet, which would be perfect. My friends from Calgary are here helping us and they found the skeleton in that area last Monday."

The Sergeant lifted his eyebrows. "I'll need to speak to them."

Gaspar blanched and then hesitantly asked, "Why?"

"Don't worry, this is just routine questioning."

Shelley quickly confirmed this, "Don't worry, it is just a normal procedure. Something that needs to be done at every inquiry."

"Should I go call Kevin and Greg?" Gaspar asked. "I hate that they need to be questioned." Then turning to Sergeant Freedmont he finished by saying, "They came here last week and finding this casket has really unnerved them."

"I am sorry, Gaspar. But it's something I can't leave undone. We all need to take a stroll to your job site and I could ask a few questions there. Like where exactly they found the casket. Dr. Brown and I can look around. Take a few pictures. This afternoon the plane is returning to pick us up and we'll want to take all the remains back to headquarters."

"Can you finish your tea and cookies, first?" Olga asked, having just sat down after serving everyone. "Or are you in a rush?"

"Absolutely we can," Sergeant Freedmont said, looking at Dr. Brown, who was preparing to get up. "We have plenty of time. This cookie is so good, and ginger is my favorite," he said as he smiled at Olga. "I know my wife wouldn't be very happy if everyone hurried away so soon after she finished serving them. How long has New Petrograd been here? I don't think I knew of its existence before, and really it isn't very far from Prince Rupert."

"It was founded by Russian immigrants fleeing persecution after the Russian revolution of 1917."

"That long! Well, in all that long history there is no record of our services being required. I checked. I guess that's a positive record to have. I believe you, Mr. Petrov, when you say that your services have seldom been needed."

A while later, as they made their way from Bob and Olga's, Gaspar felt all the village folks' eyes on them. This left him feeling very exposed and he couldn't wait to get to the job site.

"Kevin, Greg," he called, "This is Sergeant Freedmont from the Prince Rupert RCMP detachment. He needs to ask you a few questions. Dr. Brown is with him. He is the coroner. They also need to take some pictures such as where the coffin was found."

Kevin set down his hammer and called to Greg. As he was walking towards them, he said, "Certainly, sir, I expected something of the sort. How can we help?'

"Oh, my questions aren't too serious. Was the coffin buried very deep? Where there any signs of it being recently tampered with? Just questions of that nature. Then we'll look at it. Take a few pictures. Maybe make a sketch of where it is."

"Oh, but we moved it," Bob exclaimed. "That was my and Gaspar's *papa's* mistake. News like this goes through the village like wildfire and we didn't want everyone coming to look at it, so we moved it to the base of the lighthouse. The lighthouse itself has been automated, but Phil, who was the lighthouse keeper, still lives there. That was the only spot we could think of to keep it untouched. As it turns out," he said, giving a little chuckle, "it is a prime location for you to load it onto the seaplane."

Dr. Brown began to say, "But that's considered tampering with evidence—" but a look from Sergeant Freedmont squelched any further comments.

"Ideally it shouldn't have been moved, but in the absence of anyone thinking to secure this site, I can appreciate how it happened."

Then noticing their confused faces, Shelley said, "Remember I told you about the tape that crime scene officers set up to secure the area? I also mentioned I would ask the sergeant if this step could be omitted." She turned to look expectantly at Sergeant Freedmont.

"Well, we'll see. That must mean, though, that two of you have recently handled the casket?"

"Yes," Bob confirmed.

"I'm going to need to fingerprint you both. Don't worry," he said, looking at Bob's startled face, "we'll only need them for elimination purposes. Because, of course, identifying any fingerprints on both the remains and the casket is something we'll need to do. Maybe it'll give us some historical indication of whatever happened."

"Did Mr. Palmer help move it too?"

Turning to look at Gaspar, Bob smiled weakly and said, "No, Marvin just helped us by holding a torch. It would have been impossible to do otherwise."

"Since it's a skeleton and not a body, doesn't that suggest it happened a long time ago, Sergeant?" Olga ventured to ask.

"Very likely, but this early in our investigation we can't rule out anything. If it was recently tampered with it could mean many things."

"Like was it recently moved here," Shelley suggested.

"Yes," Sergeant Freedmont responded.

When the questioning was completed, Sergeant Freedmont tucked his notebook away in his shirt pocket. Then he asked Kevin and Greg to lead him and Dr. Brown down the ladder, so they could do their sketches and take pictures.

Bob winced when he thought of the rickety old ladder and then realized Gaspar was speaking to him.

"Mr. Petrov, do you think it is okay if I leave now to ask *Papa* to come to your house, so they can fingerprint him?"

"I don't see why not. I'm sure they will be busy here for a few minutes."

Gaspar left everyone and quickly drove home.

"Well, why?" Tony asked, when Gaspar said he needed to come to the Petrov house for fingerprinting. When Gaspar told him, and that it was only for elimination purposes, Tony was quite happy to cooperate. He was eager, in fact, to help.

When the seaplane returned, they were standing on the wharf with the casket ready. Sergeant Freedmont had issued sterile plastic gloves to handle it, although even he laughed and said they were probably redundant now.

As the men prepared to leave, Olga said, "I never did like going into that cellar. I didn't know why, but I just didn't. Now, these many years later, perhaps I have my answer."

The job site had indeed been roped off with the customary yellow crime scene tape. However, understanding the circumstances, Sergeant Freedmont agreed that they could continue working around it. He did ask that the area where the remains were found be left open though, in case they required anything else.

When the men had left, a tired looking Bob turned from the dock and hastened to the Borscht Kettle to open it for the remainder of the day.

Gaspar and Shelley stood and watched the seaplane until it was just a tiny dot in the sky and then they also made their way to the Kettle.

After Bob had served them, Gaspar sat slouched in a chair, leaning back with a glass of *stewler*. He was nervously turning it around in his hand. After a while he said, "I ordered this drink of fermented milk because my stomach is just wrenching. It usually helps settle it down." After a few minutes he added, "I can't stand it, Shelley, and you tell us it is only beginning."

If she thought about it, she wouldn't have responded like she did, but she didn't think. The next thing she knew, she had taken him in her arms and said, "As I explained before, it could take a very long time. This case is a monumental task. I'm quite happy I'm not working on it."

Gaspar sat up abruptly. "You are?"

"No," she said, smirking at him. "My job is right here, keeping your sanity." Then as if an afterthought, added, "And everyone else's. Come on, Gaspar, let's go get your buddies and head home. It is still afternoon, but it seems like it's been a very long day."

"The longest I've ever experienced, and I'll bet Kevin and Greg feel the same."

———

"It was awful," Shelley said dramatically to her mother the next morning. "He probably thinks I throw myself at men all the time. I just don't think I can face him. For the rest of the time I'm here I'll have to act in a professional fashion. Especially whenever I'm around him!"

"I'm sure he didn't think you threw yourself at him," June replied calmly.

"What else could he think? Because that is exactly what I did."

Marvin, who was sitting at the table reading the paper, was secretly getting a lot of amusement out of his wife and daughter's conversation. When a knock came at their door, Marvin laid down his newspaper, and looking over at his wife with a grin, said, "I didn't think we were expecting anyone, were we?"

"No, we weren't. Maybe you'd better answer it, so we all know who is there."

A few minutes later, they could hear Marvin speaking in an exaggerated loud voice, "Oh, hi, Gaspar. Shelley's in the kitchen with her mother. Go right on in."

As Gaspar entered the kitchen. June greeted him warmly. "Good morning, how are you today? I'm sure you're much better than yesterday. Shelley told us everything last night. Can you stay a while? Can I pour you a drink?"

"No, thank you, I'll only just be a minute. Yes, Mrs. Palmer, yesterday was awful. I can't imagine how I would have got through everything without Shelley. She was terrific. I just came here to thank her and to ask if she'd like to have lunch with me."

Shelley perked up and, with a huge grin on her face, replied sweetly, "I'd love to. I was just visiting with my parents. Just give me a few minutes to get ready." Without a backward glance, she raced out of the kitchen.

"Sure. I can come back in a half hour," he called to her retreating back. "I'll just be at home."

"Oh, I don't think there's any need to go home," Marvin invited. "Just wait here. I'm enjoying looking at the *Vancouver Sun* Shelley brought me. Would you like to look at a section?"

"May I have the sports, please? I haven't kept track of what's happening in the NHL since I came home."

"Okay. Sports it is."

A half hour later, as the door shut behind them, Marvin shook his head and chortled. Then looking at June, he declared, "Who would have thought! I wouldn't mind if my little girl did get serious about Gaspar. He's a fine young man. and best of all, she'd be living right here."

CHAPTER FIFTEEN

A Job in Full Force

Thursday morning, Kevin and Greg drove to the wharf in a light drizzle to receive the backhoe and the materials for the cement work. By the time they had moved everything to the job site, it was pouring.

"You know, Kevin, I'm thinking we maybe shouldn't start digging. Because we wouldn't want to cause any damage to this area the police have secured for their investigation."

"Good thinking, Greg. I agree it could be risky. Certainly, we don't want to contaminate the area. That sergeant seemed friendly, but I wouldn't like to have to tell him we did something against his orders and messed up his crime scene."

By now they had made their decision and were beginning to walk home. Despite the rain coming down in sheets, they rather enjoyed it. They had been in the village long enough that several folks recognized them and called out greetings as they scurried past.

Greg continued their conversation as they walked along. "Worse yet, we'd probably be dealing with the coroner and he certainly wouldn't be pleasant. Let's talk to Shelley and let her know we'll wait until we hear from her to resume working."

Kevin playfully nudged Greg and said, "I don't know about you, but that sounds like a job for Gaspar. I agree with you again, though—Dr. Brown sure wasn't very pleasant when he was here. I think, left to him, he would have fined, or even jailed Gaspar's dad and Mr. Petrov. Can you imagine two men who are obviously considered the backbone of this community being put in jail?"

They were warmly received by Daria as she hustled them inside. Tony hurried around getting a fire built in the fireplace. Then he patted the two closest chairs, inviting the boys to enjoy the warmth of the fire. The next thing they knew, Gaspar's mom was offering them a huge slice of warm cake and a mug.

"This sure is good, Mrs. Rosso," Kevin smiled at her.

"It is," Greg agreed. "I don't think I've had this before."

"It is called *sharlotka* cake. It's a staple on every Russian menu and instead of just regular tea I made you a traditional wintertime honey-based one called *sbiten*. I thought it was perfect for anybody coming home wet and cold."

It didn't only rain on Thursday; the rain kept up for a little over a week. Many days Kevin and Greg accompanied Gaspar as he took care of various handyman jobs. Other days they were quite content to stay home and soak up Daria's pampering.

————

Tuesday night, before heading to the Borscht Kettle for the weekly meeting, Gaspar stopped by the Palmers' to invite Shelley to go with him. She happily accepted, suggesting to her folks that they could enjoy an evening by themselves. She chose to ignore the look they gave each other. Grabbing her coat, she joined Gaspar on the porch.

As he heard the door close, Marvin commented to June, "She'd accept an invitation with him no matter where he was going."

"Really," June coyly answered him. "As I did with you whenever you invited me. And look where it got us!"

———

"Hello and welcome back," Anna said with a grin as she came over to hug Shelley. "I just knew you'd return. I could never have anticipated that this would be the reason why, though. It does sadden me."

"I agree, a person sure can't predict what is going to happen next. I'd much prefer it being for another reason, but I can't say I'm sorry I'm here."

Gaspar's opening statement was, "We really don't have much news to discuss tonight. The backhoe and supplies for the foundation arrived on the barge. It has rained every day since, delaying any work, so this week there hasn't been much progress. Shelley can maybe enlighten you about the RCMP's visit and what's happening in that regard."

"Certainly," she said. "Before I begin, though, I'd like to say that Gaspar has informed me of the plans you are working on. I quite enjoyed the coziness of the Thanksgiving gathering in the church. However, I believe your idea of expanding this room, so it will easily accommodate everyone, is excellent. I don't really feel I have much input, not knowing anything about construction. I guess when Gaspar invited me, I accepted because it gave me an evening out."

"Don't worry," Jenny said, "Only a few of the men have any experience with construction. The rest of them are here to assist wherever they can. As for us, we come to the meetings just in case there is something we can help with. So, really we are here for the same reason."

"Before I address Gaspar's request, I would like to say the reason Kevin and Greg did not want to operate the backhoe is that the sergeant has secured the area with crime scene tape. They felt the risk too great that they might mistakenly shovel dirt where it shouldn't go. As a police officer, I can appreciate their concern about doing any damage. Not everyone is so mindful.

"As for the evidence that was found there, we've met with local authorities and are following through with everything they have requested. They spoke with Kevin and Greg and looked at the scene, took pictures and sketches and removed what evidence there was. Now all we can do is wait to hear from them."

"Who do you mean by local authorities? Do you mean someone other than Mr. Petrov?" Martin wanted to know.

"Mr. Petrov was involved, but I mean an RCMP sergeant and the coroner from Prince Rupert."

"Wow, this must be big then!" Martin exclaimed.

Shelley smothered a smile before responding, "You are correct, it is big. Enormous, in fact."

The conversation slowly drifted to other things. By the time everyone was preparing to go home, more friendly chatter than any work had been accomplished.

"Thank you, Gaspar," Shelley said when they stopped in front of her parents' home. "I really enjoyed my evening."

"I'm glad. Why don't you come every week?"

Shelley looked at him with her warmest smile, and replied, "I would love that."

————

Towards the end of the following week, Shelley received word from the coroner that the examination had been completed. It was determined the person had died from a blunt force blow to the head. It had not yet been decided just how it had happened, whether it had been caused by another person or an accident. Dr. Brown did say he wouldn't need to return to the burial site. Therefore, he was giving Shelley permission to remove the crime scene tape.

Shelley explained to Gaspar as they walked over to the crime scene that he had made it clear, this was a privilege he was giving her only because of her credentials. She then went on to explain, "This means they both are still actively involved. The RCMP because it they haven't decided if it's a crime or not. The coroner because he still needs to identify the body and then see if there are any relatives who should be notified. If they can't solve it in a reasonable amount of time it may remain a cold case, which is another way of saying an unsolved mystery."

As Shelley was removing the tape, Greg was firing up the backhoe. Soon great buckets of earth were being removed.

"Actually," Greg excitedly exclaimed at dinner that night, "having a big hole nearby is great because as we dig, we have somewhere to put the earth."

"It sure is good," Kevin agreed. "It is like we can accomplish two goals at once."

"Have you noticed the weather?" Greg asked. "It's a marvel.

The rain has stopped, and I even saw a rainbow embracing the horizon."

"That is good," Gaspar agreed. "Just in time for the weekend. I know several men indicated on Tuesday that if work is being resumed, they plan on coming Saturday."

"By Saturday," Greg said, "we'll be ready to pour the cement and we sure can use some labourers. I like the days when the men come. It makes the job seem more like fun than actual work."

Slowly, week by week. they continued the construction on the new building and every Tuesday the committee gathered for a progress report. Although now that the building was being framed and dried in, what needed to be discussed was minimal. The meetings were becoming an excuse for the young adults of the village to get together and socialize for an hour. In fact, what was most often discussed now were all the activities that could happen in the extra space. As Bob went around bringing drinks, he wore a subtle smile as the plans and ideas he heard increased in their grandeur.

It was on one such evening that Anna and Alex hadn't come to the meeting. They had sent word earlier that the family was very concerned about *dedushka*. His health had recently been declining and Alex's *papa* was very troubled. His *mama* also said that, for someone who was always very vibrant, he was becoming as equally withdrawn. Alex was overheard saying his *dedushka* was shrinking away to nothing. In fact, he was worried that soon he would just shrivel and fade away.

CHAPTER SIXTEEN
Social Butterflies

It seemed to Gaspar that he and Shelley were quickly becoming New Petrograd's social butterflies. A week ago, they had been invited to John and Sandy's house one evening for supper and a few games. Tonight, they were driving to Martin and Gayle's. Anna had invited them to their place the following week. Kevin and Greg had been invited each week, but had excused themselves as being too tired. He wondered about this, because most of the time they didn't appear to be.

Was someone in the village playing matchmaker? Were his buddies in on it? Well. he didn't mind; in fact, he was secretly enjoying it.

As he drove across the village, these thoughts and a few more were rattling around in his head. He was becoming increasingly aware of her all the time. He liked how bubbly she was and loved how he felt when he was with her. He noticed how often they laughed at the same jokes. He had even thought maybe of inviting her out on a real date, but had just as quickly doused the thought. What was there to do, where was there to go other than to his friends' homes? Which brought him zooming straight back to what he was thinking a few minutes ago. Who was setting all this up?

As he was driving Shelley home later that evening, an idea popped into his mind. Why not invite her out for a drive? Maybe they couldn't travel far on these bush roads, but the benefit was that he'd have her all to himself for a few hours. The idea continued to smoulder for the five minutes it took to drive home. It grew stronger and stronger so that by the time they arrived, his mouth involuntarily opened. As he reached across the seat and placed a hand on her shoulder, he asked her. The answering yes was received not so much in words but in the brilliant smile that flashed through the darkness.

"I think it's best if I take an afternoon off work during the week. Then no one will be the wiser."

So, they arranged the date for the following Monday. Then she jumped out of the truck and sprinted across the street to her front door. Before entering the house, he noticed her looking back, and gave a friendly wave.

When he got home, Greg looked up and commented, as he came in, "You look like you had a nice evening."

Which prompted Kevin to briefly break his concentration on the chess board on the table. "Yeah, you do. In fact, you look like someone who has the cat in the bag."

Gaspar sat down in an easy chair before answering. "We had a great evening. A nice dinner of chicken *Kiev*; some good laughs. What more could a person ask for?"

Then, refusing his mother's offer of coffee, he excused himself. "I'm tired."

Once he was in bed, he began questioning what he had done. *She doesn't even live here. Do you want to get involved with someone who lives so far away?* He wasn't sure he could handle a long-distance relationship. Was he getting himself involved in another situation like Barbara? Such troubled thoughts were like bullets firing through his mind until eventually sleep came, releasing him.

For a few days Gaspar went about his daily work, sometimes deliriously happy, while at others the negative thoughts plagued him. What was a man to do? At least, he thought, he had until Monday before a decision had to be made.

Saturday was an amazing day. As he worked alongside everyone, he realized how easily Kevin and Greg had assumed the roles of foremen. They were setting up work plans, giving instructions, assisting where needed—in short, supervising. Gaspar was only too eager to fit into these new arrangements. He couldn't help but think what a good job they were doing, as he had known they would. You could tell by the way all the village men were responding to them.

Finally, at the end of the day, Kevin rang the ship's bell. Gaspar's first thoughts were, *Ship's bell? I wonder where he got it?* Then he smiled, remembering that it normally sat on the bar at the Borscht Kettle.

When he came to think of it, his buddies were taking over the Tuesday night meetings as well. This really made him proud. Being a focal point had never been his forte. He would much rather sit back and listen to others. Besides, it made total sense; they were certainly more up to date on the day-to-day happenings at the site.

When he went home on Saturday night, he had to admit to himself what a welcome relief the day had been. All day he hadn't had time to think of the questions surrounding Shelley.

On Sunday though, he realized he had resumed questioning the pros and cons of taking her out. He woke up Monday morning realizing he still didn't have an answer. What should he do? *Well,* he finally thought, *I am only taking her on a simple drive, not proposing marriage. No harm in that.*

So, that afternoon, he walked across the street and knocked on the Palmers' door. Marvin answered it and invited him in as if it was the most natural thing that Gaspar would be calling for his daughter. Even the newspaper routine was the same.

One sight of Shelley entering the kitchen clinched everything. She had taken time to curl her hair, which cascaded down her back in long blonde waves. She had artfully applied a touch of makeup, which made her eyes appear bluer than ever. She wore black jeans which she had coordinated with a fuzzy red wool sweater. One look at this vision in front of him and his heart leapt. What was the question he'd been pondering earlier? He certainly knew the answer now. The next thought flashing across his mind was, *I'm sure glad I took time to shave again before I came over.*

"Hi Gaspar," she shyly said, as she came over to him. "I just need to put on my jacket. Then I'm ready to go." His heart was treated to another one of her brilliant smiles.

They walked out together, skirting puddles from last night's rainstorm, and crossed the street to where his truck was parked.

Such fun they had, driving on the bumpy bush roads, which were now lightly covered in snow. Shelley was even finding it fun to exaggerate the bumps, laughing hilariously as she did so. He added his deep chuckles in harmony, because who could resist her enjoyment?

They laughed and talked companionably all afternoon, sharing stories of their past and of their families. When there was a moment of silence, even it was magical.

Around one o'clock, Gaspar stopped near Rushing Falls.

After helping Shelley out of his vehicle, he grabbed her hand while they walked closer to the falls.

Unlike in the summertime, only a small trickle escaped the ice that was forming on the falls. For the first time that day, Gaspar thought of the building and felt thankful that it was nearly dried in, since winter was quickly approaching. Then Shelley drew his attention back and he was just focused on her again.

As the afternoon grew dusky, they turned the truck and headed back to New Petrograd. As subtly as he could, in a village that had only four vehicles, he parked at the Kettle. Leaving Shelley, he went inside to pick up the two meals he had pre-ordered. Then they drove to the end of the wharf to eat their supper. The date he had envisioned was going like clockwork.

"This has been the loveliest afternoon, Gaspar. And to think I almost missed it."

"Almost missed it? Why? We made these plans last Thursday."

"I know, but you wouldn't believe all the questions that went through my mind after that. Did did I want to get involved with someone living so far from Vancouver? On top of that, there isn't even good access here. Then I decided, what did any of that matter? We're just going for an afternoon's drive, that's all. I like you, Gaspar. I love being in your company, and that is all that really seemed important. I knew I was attracted to you when I left last time," she said, as her words trailed off.

Then it was Gaspar's turn to admit he had his own misgivings. He confessed that it wasn't until he had seen her that morning that he'd truly let his feelings rule.

Then, taking her in his arms, he lightly kissed her. They

shared a few kisses, but mostly felt pleasure in sitting quietly holding hands. They sat that way for a long time, listening to the sounds of the sea slowly slapping against the pier and enjoying each other's company.

The one thing they both knew was that this time, when she returned to Vancouver, they would find a way to keep in touch.

CHAPTER SEVENTEEN

A Job Complete

One evening in mid-December, Kevin asked Gaspar, "How would you like to come and witness the last of the nails being driven in?"

"Are you serious?" Gaspar and Tony asked incredulously. "We wouldn't miss it for anything."

"I want to come, too," Daria said, eagerly. "This event needs a drumroll, but I'm not too sure how we can make one. It might be a little hard to do but we'll see what can be arranged. I may even finally get a ride in my son's truck. I hinted about it, what was it, six weeks ago? You remember, when you took delivery?"

Gaspar looked sheepishly at his *mama* before saying, "Absolutely I will drive you. I need to warn you, though, you'll have to share the seat with Shelley."

"Of course," Daria said. "She'll want to be there too." She resisted the urge to ruffle his hair.

Then turning his attention back to his friends, Gaspar suggested, "I personally think we need to call an impromptu meeting tomorrow night to announce this to everyone on the committee. I'm quite sure they'll all want to be there."

"I took the liberty of mentioning it to Mr. Petrov today," Kevin said, "and he said something about making it a special occasion. He plans to serve some drinks and something that sounded like *p-y-r*... on the house."

"*P-y-r?* Are you sure it isn't *p-i-r?* Because the only thing I can think of that makes sense is *pirogi*," Daria interjected. "They're puff pastries that you bake like a pie and fill with quark or cottage cheese, honey, fruit, nuts, or poppyseeds. They are very, very delicious! I can see where Bob would think of handing them out as an appetizer. I must ask him if he needs help making them, because he'll need a lot."

"Yes, I think that sounds right, don't you think, Kevin?"

Kevin nodded but continued to speak to Gaspar. "I am in favour of making an announcement—in fact I quite like that idea. I know we've been reporting on our progress at the weekly meeting, but this is something I think you should handle."

"Once we finish the actual building, I still need a few days to do the electrical work," Greg said. "If you are thinking of bringing in a plumber, this would be the time for that too."

"I have the plumber all lined up. He's just waiting for Mr. Filipov to call him on the wireless and let him know we're ready. I think the plan is that he'll board at the Katovik house while he's working here. Joe has it scheduled to bring the plumbing supplies on Thursday. It sounds like the final stages of this building are coming together perfectly."

"It sure is great how it is all coming together, with not too many days to spare before the New Year's celebration. Good job, lads," Tony said, with approval.

In order to coordinate the event into everyone's schedule, it was decided it would be held the following Saturday afternoon. Afterwards, everyone agreed it had been nothing short of amazing. It was discussed with the committee, as planned, on Wednesday night, but by noon on Thursday the entire village was aware. In fact, many of the women had offered to help Bob prepare the large number of *pirogis* that he would need.

Someone suggested that Bob should cut a ribbon to the extension. Again, many of the women had rapidly shuffled through their sewing baskets to find ribbon. Then they had quickly sewn bits and pieces of scrap ends together. The ribbon ended up being multicoloured and multisized, but it didn't seem to matter. In fact, it seemed to add to its attraction. As for the drum roll, with several pairs of hands gleefully clapping, one only needed to use a bit of imagination to hear the drums.

Bob ran out of drinks and had to ask Frank to run back to his store and bring anything he had in his supplies. At the end of the day everyone said they had a wonderful time.

Tuesday night at what everyone suspected would be the final committee meeting, Anna said, "You men have done a tremendous job. Now there is just a little more for you to do, but for us womenfolk, our job is just beginning."

When Anna received several puzzled stares, she quickly reminded them that they needed to decorate the annex for the New Year's celebration.

Several heads, even the men's, nodded in understanding,

and Sandy suggested they could get together tomorrow night at her place to come up with a plan. "First though, we need a tree," she said, as she looked pointedly at her husband.

"May I join you?" Shelley asked, a little tentatively.

"Of course, we'd be delighted to have you come," Anna and Sandy quickly replied.

"I think we all just think of you as one of us," Gayle added.

"Well, I think we need to chop down the Christmas trees. Why don't we schedule this as our wrap-up meeting? We can all go to the woods this Saturday," Alex suggested.

"I like your thinking," Nick replied. "I may even have enough money in the budget to purchase some decorations. Come and talk with me later."

CHAPTER EIGHTEEN
Celebrations Galore

By December 31, the village looked so festive with every home displaying at least one Christmas tree. Pine branches had been hung on the front doors and garlands hung in the houses.

On his final trip for the year, Joe had brought tables and chairs for the annex to the Borscht Kettle. No one confessed to ordering them, so it was suggested that maybe *Ded Moroz*, otherwise known as Father Frost, had. This seemed as good an answer as any. Each table was artfully decorated with pine boughs and colourful dishes filled with berries, nuts, and candy.

Ded Moroz and Snegurochka, his lovely Snow Maiden, (aka: John and Sandy) delivered packages for the children that the ladies from the committee had wrapped and carefully set under the three pine trees placed around the room. Squeals of delight could be heard from all parts of the room as the children opened their parcels. The girls found books, dolls, or stuffed animals in their packages. Popular items for the boys were boats, trucks and cars, or model kits.

"I imagine," Daria whispered to June, "That later tonight they'll receive parcels with clothes in them from their *roditeli*."

"Sounds right, if it's anything like our household," June laughed.

Across the room Peter was jumping in delight, while calling to Gaspar, "I've got a toolbox. It's even in my favorite colour, blue. It has a hammer, saw, wrench, measuring tape and screwdrivers. Next time, if my *papa* says I can come, I'll really be able to help you."

Three thumbs went up in a display of approval from Gaspar, Kevin, and Greg.

"It looks like you'll have a new helper soon," Greg said, smiling at Gaspar.

"You bet," Gaspar replied. "Alexander has also indicated he wants to do more work with me."

After all the gifts were delivered, the meal started. Much to June and Marvin's astonishment, in addition to the usual dishes this feast consisted of great platters of roasted pig, stuffed pig's head, sour cream hare, and lamb.

"Oh," Shelley said. "I simply must get a picture of the pig's head. My brothers will love it!"

"I agree, Shel, they will like your picture, but I reckon most of all they would love eating this feast," Marvin replied.

"Maybe we can convince them to visit us next year," June said, wistfully.

Later, as Marvin patted his stomach and was preparing to fold his napkin, trays of venison and whole fish were placed on the table. With the arrival of more food, he and Kevin looked at each other and chortled.

Kevin's cheeks were puffed out like a chipmunk's as he chewed on some roasted pig. When he could finally speak, he said to Marvin, "I don't suppose we are meant to eat something from every platter, but... well, I think that's what I've been doing. I'm sure glad Gaspar convinced Greg and I to stay."

"I have to agree," Marvin said, giving a sideways look at June. When he noticed that she was visiting with Anna and bouncing one of the twins, he visibly seemed to sigh. "I think I've also had a taste of everything that has been served."

"My mom wasn't very happy when I wrote her and said I wouldn't be home for Christmas. She made her displeasure quite plain in the letter I got back. Oh well, by next year I'm sure she'll have forgotten. Or at least she'll have forgiven me."

"You'll probably be on Santa's naughty list next year," Greg retorted, between mouthfuls. "My folks weren't pleased either. I agree, this wouldn't have been something to turn down. I think I've eaten as much food today as I cooked all last year."

"Well maybe cooked, but not eaten," Gaspar jokingly said. "That's one great thing about moving home—my *mama's* cooking. Is there anything else I can pass anyone?"

"Most certainly not. I'm finished!" Marvin said as he tossed down his napkin. Only to lift his head, throw up his hands, and chuckle. When everyone turned to look in the same direction, they too saw the huge trays of delicious looking dessert pies.

"Did Bob prepare all this?" June asked Olga, aghast.

"Oh my, no, it's a communal effort. Just like Russia Day last summer, or Thanksgiving. I guess one little difference is that Bob arranges the menu and coordinates what each person is bringing."

"I wish someone had asked Shelley and me to participate," June remarked, sadly.

Olga patted her hand, and said, "You just enjoy yourself through the Christmas traditions, my dear. Just like last summer at Russia Day. Next year will come soon enough. I'm sure by then Bob will be asking you to bring something. Isn't it lovely that this room accommodates everyone so nicely and with room to spare?"

"It sure is," June answered her, as she looked around.

Frank and Betty ate quickly before excusing themselves to go home to be with his *papa*. As they made their hasty exit, many were calling out asking how he was and giving *dedushka* their love. Frank paused long enough to say, "Thank you, I will. For now, we're just grateful he isn't getting any worse."

Then Anna and Alex came, but their faces seemed very drawn and it was difficult to tell how much they enjoyed themselves.

While the clock slowly clicked towards twelve, Phil stood and read a newspaper article which had been passed on from his *roditeli* with Christmas stories and verses in which the hero is miraculously saved from danger on Christmas Day.

Numerous other Christmas stories were recited that had also been passed down through the generations.

S Novym Godom rang throughout the evening, growing in intensity as the clock came closer to striking midnight.

For its debut event, the annex to the Borscht Kettle proved to work perfectly to everyone's satisfaction.

Later that evening, Shelley commented to Gaspar, "I think my first duty of the New Year is that I write to my boss and ask for an extension on my leave. I think I'll ask him for another six weeks."

"That will mean you plan to be here until mid-February. What happens next?"

"Well, if I haven't heard anything on the case by then, I'll have to decide what I'm going to do. Let's hope we hear something, though. An extra six weeks means I'll have been here for three and a half months, not that I'm complaining."

Soon the Palmers and Gaspar's friends learned that this was only the beginning of the holiday celebrations.

On January 7, everyone gathered at the church to celebrate the passing of the old year. Gaspar had carefully explained the tradition that Christmas Day fell on January 7 in the Julian Calendar.

Shelley and June were enchanted to hear everyone calling out words of greeting amongst themselves.

"How are you greeting each other?" June asked Marg, who was standing nearby.

"Well, the first greeting, *Xristos Voskress*, means *Christ has risen*. Then the response is, *Voistenno Voskress,* and that means *For certain Christ is here.*"

"How lovely! I like that."

Then, turning to face Marg, June haltingly attempted to give the greeting. Marg responded with "*Voistenno Voskress.*" Then, she embraced June before exclaiming, "I love your enthusiasm for learning our traditions!"

Then they proceeded to cross the room stumbling over the unfamiliar words, haltingly calling to everyone in earshot. They waited for the answering response, which was also offered with a gaiety to match their own.

After the service the Palmers had been invited to the Rosso household to share in their traditional feast of the Holy Supper. This consisted of several dishes, one to honour each of the Twelve Apostles.

Several others had also been invited—Phil and Marg, Bob and Olga, John and Sandy, and much to the delight of everyone, Anna and Uri. The twins had just turned three months. They were beginning to reach for their toys when they were held in front of them. Then they would coo delightedly, which charmed everyone.

"It sure is good to see them. Of course, we saw them from a distance at the Thankgsgiving celebration," Tony said, as he reached for Madeline.

"Oh, they look so adorable in their matching outfits," Marg said, reaching out for her great nephew.

"I agree. Matthew is quite the young man in his tiny suit and tie," Phil said, coming up behind her.

After handing Matthew to Phil, Marg left the men to entertain the babies. Then she joined the women as they busied themselves with the final preparations for supper.

Shelley and June were further enlightened in the Russian traditions when they went to sit at the table. Various symbolic features were carefully explained, including the placing of hay under the tablecloth in memory of the manger in which the Holy Child was placed by His mother after His birth. Then there was grain haphazardly tossed in the straw representing the abundance of Christ's coming. Lastly, Daria explained that even her *mama's* linen tablecloth, which had been passed down through the family, was used to represent the swaddling clothes Christ was wrapped in.

Marvin and Gaspar's buddies showed much more interest in the meal placed before them. Although June wondered how they could, knowing how much her husband had consumed in the last week.

Tony explained to them that the meal consisted of twelve courses, which symbolized the twelve Apostles. "Daria and several of the ladies here tonight have prepared the twelve fasting foods. They are barley, honey, stewed prunes, *pierogi*, sauerkraut, potatoes, lima beans, garlic, Lenten bread, mushrooms, soup and salt."

Gaspar went on to explain that they were foods which honoured Mother Earth. "These are reminders to us that life is both bitter and sweet, and that the work of each day throughout the year is required to truly celebrate Christ's coming."

"Thank you for sharing so much of your customs," June said, as they were preparing to leave.

"Well our evening doesn't end here," Daria replied. "We would like to invite you again to the church for an all-night vigil. Don't feel bad if you don't want to come. Or for that matter, don't stay very long. After all, not everyone does."

"Oh, I want to go," Shelley heartily replied.

"Me too," June said, and so, reluctantly, Marvin came along.

———

The holiday season consisted of still one more holiday and on January 13, everyone trudged through the snow for the final celebration of the season: New Year's coming. This time the Palmer family was thrilled at the pure fun everyone was having.

Led by Marie, the children went from house to house singing carols. Whether they were on or off key, it didn't matter. Afterwards, when everyone gathered on the wharf, the children gaily danced, often falling in their *mamas'* laps at the end. Then the strongmen of the village competed against each other in the chopping of wood. Kevin and Greg, upon realizing what was happening, jostled each other as they joined the line behind Alexander.

When the long line of men who had entered the competition was finished, Martin, who was emceeing the event, urged every family to take some of the wood home for their fireplaces.

As the afternoon turned into evening, the crowd began to amble towards the Borscht Kettle, where Bob had another assortment of hot drinks and snacks ready.

As if he had planned it as a grand encore to the holiday season, the most exciting occurrence came when Phil stood and, pulling Marg close into his embrace, announced that they were engaged.

———

The next day, as Marvin took down the tree, Shelley lay on the living room couch groaning. "This sure has been fun, but I believe I've put on ten pounds or more. I used to feel stuffed with our Christmas celebrations, but they were never like this."

"Well," Marvin told her, "you should have taken Daria's advice and fasted beforehand. She knew what was coming."

"I know," she said smiling at her father. "It seems to me, though, I recall your plate was often piled pretty high."

"Don't remind me."

"Shelley, earlier Daria was teaching me to cook some Russian dishes," June said, coming into the living room. "Would you like to join us?"

"I'd love to. Anna is going to teach me some Russian words, too."

"I think everyone who worked on the building project is feeling at loose ends now," June said.

"Talking about loose end," Shelley said, "Gaspar and I have been thinking about the time passing, and there's still no word regarding the identity of the skeleton. We've talked about it often when we've gone driving. I'm aware that Sergeant Freed-mont came and looked around one afternoon. I don't think he found anything that he could use for his investigation. I imagine that from his perspective, it remains a cold case."

———

On January 17, most of the committee and a few other village folks gathered on the wharf. Ignoring the biting wind driving the snowflakes, they waved goodbye to Kevin and Greg as they left New Petrograd for Vancouver on Joe's barge.

CHAPTER NINETEEN
Confessions

It was towards the end of January that Dr. Brown brought shattering news. They had identified the skeleton as 28-year-old Arlene Green.

"But that isn't possible," Bob said, his voice breaking with emotion. "My *roditeli* told me the reason she stopped coming is because she had moved away."

"That's right," Olga breathed. "My mama told me she got married, so it only made sense she might have moved away. I remember it so well, because my *mama* and I had fun looking at magazine pictures and visualizing her in one of the wedding dresses. I thought she was so pretty. Then Mrs. Gilbert started to come. She was older and not nearly as much fun as Miss Green was. I didn't care if I ever saw her."

"Are you sure you have identified her properly?" Bob asked.

Dr. Brown's scornful look was answer enough, even without speaking. "Absolutely. We looked back in police records at people were reported missing forty to sixty years ago. Most of them, of course, had been solved a long time ago. Once we had short-listed from the cold cases some potential missing persons, we started considering other clues. There were still some teeth in the face of the skeleton that we could use to compare with dental records. Everything pointed in one direction."

Bob, in a shaky voice, finally asked the questions on everyone's mind. "She was here all this time? How can that be? Who would have killed her? Why would they have? Everyone loved her."

Dr. Brown repeated that she had died from blunt force trauma to the back of her head. The reason why had still not been determined. "I'm now attempting to locate any relatives she might have had who are still living. It's reasonable to suspect her parents are deceased. Do any of you recall her mentioning siblings we may be able to locate?"

"Of course not," Olga haughtily answered him. "We were only children when she visited."

As the news spread around the village, others like Phil, Marg, Daria, Betty, and Frank shared stories that seemed to correspond with these. In fact, that Friday at fish and chips night it seemed to be the only subject on people's minds.

On the following Thursday night, the Rossos and Palmers got together at June and Marvin's. The teams had just been set for a game of Trivial Pursuit—Gaspar, June, and Marvin against Shelley, Tony, and Daria—when a knock came at the door.

Looking at Gaspar, Marvin wondered, "Who can that be?"

"Well, if you don't answer it, we won't know, love."

A few minutes later Marvin said, his voice laced with surprise, "Frank, how nice to see you. Come in. Where's Betty?"

But Frank answered, "I've come to see Shelley. Is she here?"

"Yes, she is home. She's in the living room. The Rossos are

here to and we were just starting to play a game. I will call her, but please, come in."

Shelley, who had obviously heard the conversation, was already coming towards them, Gaspar following a few steps behind her. "Mr. Yusperov, what can I do for you? How is *dedushka*?"

At the mention of *dedushka,* Frank paled and he stuttered out, "Could you come to my place? Bob will be there. It's important."

"Of course. Is everything okay? I'll just grab my down coat."

"I'll drive you both," Gaspar said, taking his keys out of his pocket while reaching into the closet for his coat with the other hand.

As the front door closed a confused babble arose amongst everyone.

"What would Frank want with Shelley?"

"And this late at night..."

"Frank said Bob would be there too..."

"She may have made a good guess, thinking it's Frank's *Papa*. Oh, I do hope he hasn't taken a turn for the worse."

An hour later, when Shelley and Gaspar returned, they found their *roditeli* sitting around drinking coffee. The game lay discarded at one end of the coffee table. Four heads eagerly looked up.

"Oh, it is so good that you're home," June said, as she hurried to greet them. "What ever did Frank need you for?"

However, all Shelley would say was, "I can't talk about it. It's just the most shocking thing I have ever heard."

The following morning, Shelley was up early. She hastened to the lighthouse to ask Mr. Filipov to contact Sergeant Freedmont and ask him to get in touch with Dr. Brown. "Please invite them to come as soon as possible. Your message should include we have a breakthrough on their case NP-100."

When the seaplane flew in later that day, with both the Sergeant and Dr. Brown aboard, Shelley met them at the dock alone.

"I am so glad you could respond to my message on such short notice. Mr. Petrov and his wife will meet us at the Yusperov home, where the urgency of my request will be explained."

"All I read was that you have a solution to the case. I didn't need anything more to book our seaplane," Sergeant Freedmont said.

"I agree. It couldn't be better timing," Dr. Brown added. "In just a few days I leave on my winter vacation. Mark my words, though, you had better not be wasting our time. I don't have time for any messing around."

"Oh, after you've heard this confession, I think you'll agree the case is solved. What Sergeant Freedmont is going to do—well, let's say I'm glad it isn't my case. Here we are now."

Shelley could hear Frank calling his *papa* as soon as she knocked on the door. Then it was quickly opened, and they were ushered inside.

As she stepped inside, Shelley introduced the three Yusperovs to Sergeant Freedmont and Dr. Brown. Then she said, "Of course, you have already met Mr. and Mrs. Petrov." Then she hugged Betty, who looked as if she was visually shaken and as though she hadn't slept much the night before.

"Yes, it's good to see you again," Sergeant Freedmont said to Bob and Olga. "Very nice to meet you folks," he said, warmly as he shook everyone's hands.

"Please have a seat," Betty invited, as she carried a big pot of tea to the table.

Olga quickly took the teapot from Betty and began pouring. "Betty, do you have any cookies, or anything?" she asked.

"Well no, I really don't. This is all so unexpected. After *Papa's* confession to us, things have moved really quickly."

"If I'd only thought, I could have brought something."

"Don't worry, we don't need anything," Sergeant Freedmont told them. "I am curious though, to hear why Shelley asked us to come right away."

Frank began, "The reason we, Betty and I, had Shelley invite you here today is that my *papa* has something to tell you. Before he does, though, I'd just like to say that this decision was made by our founding fathers not long after they arrived from Russia."

"What has all this to do with our case?" Dr. Brown asked impatiently.

"Just that they were afraid of the authorities. *Papa,* now tell everyone what you told me last night."

Dedushka did not look at anyone in the room but seemed to be looking at something far away. When he finally began to speak, it was hard to understand because of his broken accent. In little more than a whisper, he began, "I think it was sometime in the early thirties. That seems about right because Frank was perhaps ten. Isabel, she was around eight. Yes, I think Steven might have been five and baby Anastasia was still in Betty's arms."

Dr. Brown cleared his throat and started rhythmically tapping the floor.

"*Papa.*"

Looking out from under thick brows, his dark eyes glanced at Frank, and then he continued, "What I have to tell you, my story is really very simple. Miss Green was our district nurse at the time. The children all loved her. In the summertime, when she came, they would follow her around like lambs."

"Mr. Yusperov, do you think you could focus? That is all very interesting, but not really to the point," Dr. Brown demanded.

After a pregnant pause, *dedushka* continued, "Yes. Yes. I guess as Frank said, we were afraid of the authorities."

Taking *dedushka's* gnarled hand in his own, Sergeant Freedmont kindly asked, "Why were you afraid of the authorities?"

"Well, because when Miss Green fell leaving the Katovik home and hit her head, Pavel wasn't home. So Yulia sent their son Roman over to Vasily Filipov's home. Pyotr and Vasily Filipov hurried over and carried Miss Green into the house and put her to bed. Then, when Yulia went in a half hour later, she found her dead. This time she went herself to Pavel's because she didn't want to tell her children. We didn't understand why she was dead. We didn't know what to do, and we were very worried that Yulia would be accused of something. So, we had a meeting amongst ourselves.

"It was decided to just bury her here. You see, we didn't want anyone outside of the village knowing she had died. We especially didn't want our children to know," he said, as he looked at Frank. "Pyotr Filipov and I built a crude coffin and we laid her in the community cold storage space. We all gathered around that evening and said a few prayers. It was really all very nice..." he concluded, with another faraway look on his deeply lined face. Then he haltingly finished. "I guess I haven't felt very well since her skeleton was found by those boys."

Dr. Brown had stopped the incessant tapping of his foot and was now looking at Sergeant Freedmont expectantly.

"You sure haven't been well, *Dedushka*," Betty said kindly, embracing him. "You've given us all such a scare."

After a while, Sergeant Freedmont spoke. "*Dedushka*, that is quite the tale. I admit, in my thirty years working on the Force, I have not heard anything like it. To be honest, I'm not sure what to do next. I'd like to do some research to see if there has ever been a similar case recorded anywhere and what recommendations they followed. Are there any others of your founding fathers alive who can confirm your story?"

"No, sir," Frank proudly answered. "My *papa* is the last of his generation."

"Just thinking out loud, I'm sure factoring in your age, and that it was an accident that caused her demise, will be taken into consideration. Your only crime is in not reporting an acci-dental death. Everyone did make a poor decision there. We members of the Royal Canadian Mountain Police are not to be feared. I hope you know that now."

After news of the confession filtered down through the village, the residents went about in disbelief. Some even wondered if *dedushka*, in his poor health, had become delusional.

A week went past, and Shelley still hadn't heard anything from the RCMP. She was secretly feeling quite strained as the days went by. She really didn't want to ask for another exten-sion on her leave of absence. Not with the case being all but solved.

When, finally, she did receive word, it was asked if they could hold a meeting where everyone would be present. Of course, that meant the Borscht Kettle. Sergeant Freedmont flew in himself and was all smiles. As they may their way from the dock, he cheerfully greeted everyone he saw.

When a crowd had assembled, Bob cleared his throat and a hush settled over the gathering. He quickly introduced Sergeant Freedmont and then stepped aside.

Sergeant Freedmont began by telling them he had done his research and had not found a similar case on record. He had then discussed his conclusion with the staff sergeant in charge of the General Investigations Section, which dealt in suspicious deaths. The decision was to not take any action against *dedushka*.

Loud cheers went up. Those standing near *dedushka* lightly began thumping him on the back and Betty feared he might fall over.

As he shook *dedushka*'s hand, the sergeant said, "Admittedly, I can say now those were my initial thoughts. It seemed though I shouldn't be too hasty, maybe sleep on it, and do some research. After all that process, it seemed clear that this is the only conclusion I could come to."

Shelley didn't think anyone was still listening to him.

Later that evening. as Shelley and Gaspar were walking Sergeant Freedmont back to his seaplane, Shelley asked, "I couldn't help but notice your uniform. Your sleeve now has four chevrons on it. Does this mean you got a promotion?"

"Yes, I am now a Staff Sergeant. There is a possibility that I'll be transferred, although I sure hope not. I like it here."

"Congratulations, sir," Gaspar said.

"Yes, congratulations," Shelley said. "I sure hope that you're not transferred. I feel comfortable leaving here now that everyone in New Petrograd knows you're just a call away. They're in good hands."

After that, *dedushka's* health began to improve immensely. In no time he was back to his vibrant self.

"I guess with the case being solved, I need to return to Vancouver," Shelley sighed on Saturday night, as she was curled up against Gaspar.

"I figured you'd be saying that soon, even though I didn't want to hear it," Gaspar said, sadly.

Then he reached into his jacket pocket and brought out a jeweller's box.

"What's this?" she asked, with a startled look.

"Open it and see."

She did, and her face lit up. Inside was a beautiful amethyst bracelet. "Oh," she whispered, on an indrawn breath. "Thank you, Gaspar. It is stunning and it's my birthstone. How did you know?"

"I wanted to give you something to remember me by before you left. I admit, I was quite pleased that afternoon when we shared our birthdays. This proved to be handy when I was thinking of getting you something. I have to confess, though, I had to ask your *mama* what February's birthstone was."

Then she extended her arm towards him, so he could put it on. "I will wear it with pride."

Then they sealed it with a kiss.

CHAPTER TWENTY

Epilogue

Early June

The extension on the Borscht Kettle was being enjoyed by all the citizens of New Petrograd. On Mondays the ladies gathered for craft night. Tuesdays the committee continued to use it just to get together and socialize. In the winter, on Wednesday nights the men came to enjoy darts or other games. Thursday nights it had become a drop-in night for whoever wanted to come, and on Fridays, fish and chips night, it was most appreciated because it had reduced the waiting time for a table to nil.

However, nothing was like the fever that was growing in the village as the date of Phil and Marg's wedding approached. The couple had planned on an intimate wedding in the lantern room at the lighthouse. Just themselves and their immediate families, with Bob and Daria as witnesses. Anyone who spoke to Phil prior to the wedding would hear him chuckle and say, "I'm not sure how all those people are going to fit, but as long as there is room for Marg and me and Father Nikolas, I'm happy."

Don and Brad, with Cheryl and their baby, Eric, had arrived home a week before the wedding. Along with the boys' childhood friend, Gaspar, they had been busy renovating their *mama*'s home for after the wedding.

Marianne and Mary Ellen arrived from Vancouver on the Thursday just before the wedding. The day of the wedding, the girls rose early and crept out of the lighthouse, making their way to the meadow to pick wildflowers for bouquets for Marg and Daria. Plus, they needed several more flowers to make boutonnières for the men. As they went, they talked happily amongst themselves of their *papa*'s wedding. Turning a corner, they almost bumped into a woman. Her arms were already laden with flowers. They would have just excused themselves and kept on going, but she looked at them closely before smiling.

"You must be Phil's daughters."

"We are," one of the girls said. "This is Marianne, and I'm Mary Ellen. We're picking flowers for Mrs. Rosnokova and Mrs. Rosso. And of course, *Papa* and Uncle Bob, too, but they will be easy enough to make."

"I'm pleased to meet you. I'm June Palmer. my husband Marvin and I moved here last year. If I may, I'd be delighted to go with you. Here, have a look and see if anything I've already picked will be suitable."

June gently laid her armful down and the twins squatted beside the pile of flowers to browse.

"What do you think, Marianne? I know *papa* has always loved daisies. Maybe we could make boutonnières out of a few of them."

"I think he would like that," her sister answered. "Maybe we could use daisies for the bouquets and something pink for a bit of colour."

"What about echinacea?" June asked. "They are a daisy-like flower. I think they would look quite lovely together. I have some growing in the greenhouse my husband built for me this past winter. I also have some purplish violas in my garden. They would make a lovely contrast. Why don't you follow me home and then I can help you arrange them?"

"Thank you," both girls said in unison and then Marianne added, "But we don't want to be a bother."

"Bother me? Not at all. I've been wondering what I could do for the happy couple and couldn't think of anything. I'm so glad I ran into you—this is just perfect."

"Oh, could you? We really don't have any idea what we are doing. We just wanted to do something for Mrs. Rosnokova, so we offered to get her flowers."

"She has made our *papa* so happy," Marianne added.

"You know. Mary Ellen, we can't keep calling her Mrs. Rosnokova for much longer."

"I know, I've thought about that. Mama doesn't seem right, but Marg? I don't know."

"Well, we can't call her Mrs. Filipov," and both girls chuckled heartily at the thought.

"I agree, I don't know, either. I guess we'll just have to ask *Papa*. Come to think of it, I wonder what Brad and Don have decided to call our *papa*. Maybe we should also ask them."

Walking past the shops towards her home, June had to smile to herself listening to the girls discussing their dilemma. After awhile though, June invitingly said, "Now tell me a bit about yourselves."

The remainder of the way to the old Pagadon house, the girls chatted happily away about their life in the city.

An hour later the two girls emerged from the Palmers', each carrying a box Marvin had prepared for them to carry the flowers. "Oh, thank you so much. I think the flowers turned out just perfect. And thank you also for the tea and cake," Mary Ellen said.

"Yes, thank you for the treats," Marianne chimed in. "These flower arrangements turned out much better than if we had tried to do them on our own."

"We'd better hurry now, Marianne, to take them to Mrs. Rosnokova and get back to the lighthouse in time. 'Bye. Thank you, again."

———

It was a stunning afternoon, the birds adding a delightful twittering as if heralding everyone and directing them to the lighthouse.

Phil remarked to Bob, as they stood waiting in front of Father Nikolas, "I really can't quite believe that after all these years, I have slept almost my last night here. Marg and I will have tonight of course, and then tomorrow afternoon Johnny Eagle Feather will be coming for us."

"Marg told me," Bob said. "Mind you, she said it's a secret that you are leaving right away. She said your plans are to spend a week in Toronto visiting Brad and his family, then come back to Vancouver to visit your girls."

"Yes. We both agreed it would make a perfect honeymoon. Marg can hardly wait to go shopping in a mall with Cheryl. She gets all excited just thinking about what it will be like. At the end of those two weeks, we still look forward to joining everyone in Seattle for the cruise to Alaska."

"We'll be waiting for you, all right. It will be just great, a retirement cruise to remember—Tony and Daria, Marvin and June, Frank and Betty, and Olga and I. Speaking of which, I can't tell you how excited Olga is that Marianne is moving home to take over the teaching position in September."

"I agree, it sure put the icing on my cake. If I was any happier, I'd burst."

Then, as the first few strains of the wedding march began to play, they turned their attention to the back where Daria and then Marg would soon appear. When Marg reached the front, Father Nikolas handed the bride and groom each a lighted candle to hold during the ceremony.

"Dearly beloved, we are gathered today..." Father Nikolas began.

As Marg and Phil repeated the familiar vows, Father Nikolas reached between them with one solid white candle, which he held there. He then instructed them to use their smaller candles to light it. Once it was lit, he instructed them to snuff out their individual ones. Then Phil and Marg held the larger candle together, signifying oneness. Daria and then Bob each produced rings so the bridal couple could place them on the ring finger of the right hand. A common cup was produced and while together they drank from it, Father Nikolas offered a blessing.

"For in the hope and wish that your joys will be doubled, and your sorrows halved, because they will be shared." Then Father Nikolas pronounced them man and wife, to the cheers of their guests.

After the ceremony finished, Bob gave Phil a thump on the

back and said, "Let me be the first to congratulate you, old chum." Then he turned and wrapped his sister in a hug.

Olga rushed to her sister-in-law and hugged her. "The service was so beautiful. I just know you and Phil are going to be so happy!"

"Yes," Daria agreed, embracing her with teary eyes. "You will. Marg, you simply look stunning today, doesn't she, Olga?"

"I agree. I also was admiring your dress. It suits you so well."

"Thank you, my dears. You know, I had Betty order me a new dress. It was quite pretty, but nothing special. Earlier I had noticed this suit in a bridal magazine recommended for mature brides. I immediately fell in love with it, but felt there was no way to order one. I had written Cheryl and I guess I told her about it because the other day she called me into their bedroom and surprised me with it. How she knew my size I don't know, because I'm sure my son wouldn't have been much help."

"Excuse me," Phil said playfully from where he still stood beside his wife, "Cheryl sure did an amazing job I'd say. I was just going to tell you that before these two ladies approached you. My love, you do look wonderful." He took her in his arms to give her a huge hug and kiss.

"*Papa,* be careful of her flowers. You are going to crush them," Mary Ellen cried.

"Yes," Marianne added, "We want them to stay nice for the pictures."

Smiling, Phil and Marg, moved a little apart from each other, but still stood holding hands.

"You look very dapper yourself, Phil, my dear." Marg said, giving him a hug before looking at his daughters with a guilty smile.

"Both of you look fabulous," Brad said as he and Cheryl, who was holding a squirming Eric, approached them. "I think you look even younger than you did the last time I came home, *Mama*."

"My thoughts exactly," Don agreed as he also came near them. "I heard Mary Ellen's comment," he chuckled. "I won't give you a hug, *Mama*, until after the pictures."

He turned and shook Phil's hand. "I think you've already been good for each other. I have to say, when *Mama* first wrote me that she was dating, I was a little concerned, but being home this week has eliminated all my doubts."

"*Mama*, I overheard you talking about your wedding suit." Cheryl laughed. "I didn't just guess, and no, Brad had nothing to do with it. I had a very good informant who happens to be in the room right now, but that is as much as I'm going to say. You look just as I anticipated when I bought it." Giving Phil a hug, she finished by saying, "And you do have a very handsome groom."

After a brief pause, Phil said, "I know Marg and I had earlier decided we wanted to go into the meadows to take pictures, but it just occurred to me that I'd like do some off the gallery deck as well. After all, this old lighthouse has been my home for many years."

"Whatever you like, honey," Marg replied as she leaned towards him. "We can do them both places. After all, we can do what we like on our day."

Tony went downstairs to alert Nick, who had offered to be their official photographer, of the change in plans. Then amidst the tremendous view of green forests on one side and the ocean, fringed with white lace, on the other, they posed. After an hour everyone went to the meadow to finish taking their pictures—those same meadows that Phil had looked over for so many years and appreciated. Daisies, bleeding heart, salmonberry, and flowering currant seemed to put on an extra display, even though the spring flowers would soon be fading and the summer flowers were only budding.

While they were there Olga produced a balloon with the Rosnokova name in it so Marg could release it into the sky.

"Here," Tony said as they came back from the meadows, "Get into my truck for a ceremonial drive around town."

They hadn't gone very far when Phil remarked, "Tony, what's that noise? I think there is something wrong with your truck."

"Oh no, there isn't," Tony replied as he laughed gleefully. "It's just the rattling of all those tin cans Gaspar tied to the back last night."

They stopped for a few minutes at the church so Marg and Phil could go to the cemetery. In keeping with Russian tradition, they wanted to make a tribute by laying both bouquets at Millie and Merle's graves.

As they were leaving, Marg said, "I feel so much better about doing this. At my age I'm certainly not into throwing my bouquet. Goodness me, I'd probably end up putting my back out."

"Well, I don't know. I think my girls were talking about who would catch it." Phil replied with a smile.

"Then they will just have to settle for taking a piece of the broken china home to dream on."

When at last the ride finished, and none too soon, Marg thought, they were in front of the Borscht Kettle. As they climbed out of the truck, Phil noticed the JUST MARRIED sign and pulling Marg tight against his side, he pointed it out.

"Oh," Marg exclaimed, "that is nice. Who made it? I would love to keep it."

"I think maybe our boys did more than renovations at your house last week. When this day is done, it's yours," Bob said with a smile. "Of course, later I have to drive you back to the lighthouse."

"Oh no, you don't," Phil said. "I think Marg and I can find our own way back just fine."

Going inside, they were loudly greeted by a mob of people cheering for them, as everyone in the village had been invited to the reception.

Martin, who was the *tamada*, or master of ceremonies, attempted, rather unsuccessfully, to organize everyone into a receiving line. When some semblance of order had been achieved, he then asked their four children to perform the customary duties of the parents. Standing together, they each presented them with some bread or salt. Mary Ellen and Don then each offered a blessing. The next few minutes seemed pandemonium as cameras clicked in every direction and the younger folk enthusiastically threw seeds of grain, candies, and coins so the couple would know happiness and prosperity.

Once everyone was seated, Martin announced the first toast, *"Za-Molodykh!"* Cheers to the couple that is presently getting married.

And as the crowd cheered, Alexander started shouting, *"Gor'ko."*

It was quickly picked up by others. *"Gor'ko, Gor'ko, Gor'ko."* The walls on every side seem to reverberate with the chant.

"Whatever is happening?" June asked Betty, who was sitting beside her.

"You just watch," Betty replied as she also picked up the chant.

Then Marvin hesitantly picked it up. After giving him a

quizzical look, June smiled at him and, shrugging, gave a little titter before she also joined in.

Then Phil and Marg reluctantly stood and kissed.

The room erupted with merriment as everyone began another chant, "One, two, three—" and they were just starting to count *Four* when everyone realized Phil and Marg had sat down. The chant begin again, *"Gor'ko, Gor'ko, Gor'ko."*

But the bridal couple remained firmly seated and laughing, Phil said, "I'm an old man and Marg isn't that young either. We need to catch our breaths. Please can we just settle for having dinner?"

This comment evoked evoked loud guffaws from the crowd.

Betty turned to June and explained, *"Gor'ko* means the wine is bitter. The wish is to have the bride and groom kiss to sweeten it."

"Ah," June replied. "That is why people weren't pleased that Phil and Marg sat down so soon."

"Exactly."

"Well, my wine must have been sweetened in those first counts because I'm not complaining," Marvin said as he swirled his wine around in his glass before taking another sip.

In response to Phil's request, the committee members all went into action. Soon great platters of roasted pig, goose and apples, and sour cream hare appeared as well as dishes like Olivier salad, *draniki*, caviar, and *pelmeni*.

June turned to Marvin and kindly suggested he control himself and not overindulge like he had at New Year's.

"I'm just taking one or two bites of everything," Marvin answered as he smiled at his wife.

Smiling back at him, June replied, "Well, make sure you can count."

Then Martin was back at the microphone commenting on the amazing meal and suggesting that everyone show their appreciation to the kitchen. By the sound of all the loud cheers, everyone agreed with the sentiment.

He then announced the first game that was going to be played. Phil was blindfolded and then Marg and five other women lined up. As he was led down the row by Frank, the object was for him to guess which one was his bride. Phil went down the line, touching a hand, or a leg. He hesitated for a few minutes in front of the second woman... but continued until finally choosing the fourth.

"Right," Marg said gleefully, obviously pleased as she quickly took off his blindfold. Then it seemed they didn't need anyone calling *Gor'ko* as they kissed.

Many started noisily thumping the table as several of the men took up a chant, "Phil, Phil, Phil."

"Now Mrs. Rosnokova ... no, I mean Mrs. Filipov," Martin said, "the ladies present would like to evaluate how good a housewife you are. An area in front of the head table has been cleared, the tables and chairs moved against the wall. I will count to three, and then you start sweeping it."

Already there was a mess of money thrown on the floor but, as she swept, guests continued to throw more.

Finally, Martin solemnly declared that Mrs. Filipov was indeed a good housewife.

In answer, Phil, smiling at his bride as he took steps to join her, said with all seriousness, "Now, that is a relief."

Everyone clapped and the women yelled a collective, "Congratulations, we knew you could do it!"

"Now that Mrs. Filipov has cleaned an area for us, perhaps the bride and groom would like to have the first dance."

As Phil whirled Marg around the dance floor, he whispered

in her ear, "How would you like to disappear after we've had this dance?"

"I think that a perfect idea. After all, we can excuse ourselves by saying we need to be up early to catch our flight."

As they were concluding the dance, Phil guided her towards the door.

"Look, they're escaping," Alexander called out. "They haven't cut the Russian Honey Cake yet. That's what I've been waiting for and drooling over all night."

The last thing some folks at the reception overheard as the couple raced towards the door was Phil saying, "Marg, Alexander is right, we didn't cut our cake. I guess my idea wasn't such a good one. Let's go back." and he began to turn.

"Oh, no we're not."

"Not even for *medovik torte*? I can just taste the walnuts sprinkled in the mounds of sour cream."

"I'll get Olga to bake us a cake when we come home." Marg said as her voice trailed off into the night.

Everyone watching them waited, but after a few minutes of seeing their shadows lengthen as they continued walking away, it was apparent that they had no intention of coming back. Several folks called out *good-bye, happy honeymoon* or *safe honeymoon* to the retreating couple.

"What a hoot,' Bob chortled as he turned away from the door. "I must say, leaving your wedding before you cut the cake is a new one on me—in fact, it may be the first in history. I don't think they'll need to stomp on any china to know who has the upper hand in this marriage."

Laughing, Mary Ellen followed Bob in and swiftly walked across to where the small table was holding the cake. She began cutting it. Don soon joined her and began serving it; calling to his brother to come help as well. Soon both Brad and

Marianne_as well as some_other guests were handing out small pieces of cake, chuckling as they did so with the other guests.

As for the long-distance relationship? Well, if anyone had asked June or Daria about Shelley and Gaspar that evening, they would have received the same response from both: "It's progressing along just fine."

PART TWO

Recipes

SBITEN

"I am so happy my mom suggested I join her and you, Mrs. Rosso, for cooking lessons," Shelley said. "They will be a great distraction while I'm waiting to hear from the RCMP Sergeant Freedman, or the coroner, Dr. Brown."

"We are so very happy to have you join us, dear." Daria handed her a mug filled with hot liquid. "Kevin and Greg enjoyed this tea so much when they would come home tired and cold from a long day at work."

Since the 12th century, *sbiten* has been consumed as a traditional wintertime honey-based beverage. It was originally served from copper samovars by the *sbitenshchik* or *sbiten* makers, who brewed it on street corners and sold it to the eager and frost-bitten public.

In the 19th century it fell out of favour as tea and coffee grew in popularity. However, recently a renewed interest is growing for this old-time drink.

Like mead and *medovukha* (a cheaper, faster version of mead), *sbiten* is made with honey, water, spices, and jam. The key to excellent *sbiten* is good quality honey and spices. As you might expect, the ratios of these ingredients depend on the family making the drink.

The word *sbiten* comes from the Russian verb *sbit*, which means *to beat* and refers to the herbs and spices being pounded in a mortar.

INGREDIENTS

- 1/2 cup honey
- 1 tablespoon whole cloves
- 3 cinnamon sticks (tip: crack into several pieces)
- 1 teaspoon ground ginger
- 16 ounces blackberry jam
- 10-1/4 cups water (or red wine)
- 1/4 teaspoon ground nutmeg
- Optional: 1 mint leaf
- Optional: 2 dried chili peppers

DIRECTIONS

Combine all the ingredients together, including the two optional ones (if using) in a medium saucepan. Using medium heat, slowly bring the mixture to a boil, stirring frequently until the honey and jam completely dissolve. Remove from heat.

For this last step, the *sbiten* should be at room temperature. Strain the liquid through cheesecloth (you may find you need to press on the solids).

Pour into an airtight container or bottle. A 750 ml bottle should be the correct size for this amount of *sbiten*. Refrigerate and reheat when serving.

. . .

As June, Shelley, and Daria poured themselves a cup to enjoy, Daria said, "There are many recipes for *sbiten*. In this one, the proportion of jam to honey is higher. Other recipes have as much as two cups of honey and only 2 tablespoons of jam. You can also add red wine, vodka, or brandy to the other ingredients if you choose. But I like this recipe best, just as it is."

DRANIKI

(Potato Latkes)

"Draniki are super simple to make and only take ten minutes to put together, with another twenty minutes to cook," Daria said to Shelley as she got out the food processor. "While they're cooking, bring out a bowl of applesauce and another one of sour cream, and in 30 minutes you are ready to enjoy. I usually find I need a double batch."

INGREDIENTS

- 4–5 large potatoes, peeled and cut in quarters
- 1 medium onion
- 1 garlic clove, peeled
- 2–3 tablespoons flour
- 1.5 teaspoon salt
- 1/8 teaspoon ground black pepper
- 1/4 cup oil

DIRECTIONS

Put all the ingredients in a food processor. Pulverize them until the batter has no large chunks. This step usually takes approximately 4 minutes.

Heat only a couple of tablespoons of oil in a skillet, and add a large spoonful of the batter. Cover with lid. Brown on one side for about 3–4 minutes and then turn. Turn and brown on the other side.

Repeat step 2 until all the batter is finished. Transfer to a serving plate and serve with sour cream or apple sauce.

Yields approximately 16–20 *draniki*.

RASSOLNIK SOUP

Beef, Barley, and Pickle Soup

INGREDIENTS

- 12 cups water
- 1 pound lean beef cut into bite-sized pieces
- 1/4 cup barley rinsed
- 1/2 tablespoon salt + more to taste
- 3 medium potatoes, diced
- 1 carrot, thinly sliced
- 6 baby pickles / 3 adult pickles or 1-1/2 cups diced
- 4 tablespoons olive oil
- 1 more carrot, grated
- 1 onion, finely diced
- 2 celery sticks, finely sliced
- 1 tablespoon tomato paste or ketchup
- 2 tablespoons dill (optional, but very nice)
- 2 bay leaves
- 1/2 teaspoon freshly ground black pepper
- Sour cream (optional) and extra dill to serve

DIRECTIONS

Add 12 cups water, beef, barley and salt to taste to a soup pot or other large pot. Partially cover with the lid and heat for 30 minutes. Be sure to skim off any impurities that rise to the top, as you want your soup clear.

Sautee pickles in 1 tablespoon oil for a few minutes on medium/high heat.

Add pickles, potatoes, and sliced carrots to the pot and cook for an additional 10 minutes.

While these ingredients are cooking, begin your *mirepoix* aka *zazharka*.

ZAZHARKA

Grate carrot and slice celery, and set them aside for a few minutes.

Add 3 tablespoons of olive oil to a large skillet and sauté onion for approximately 2 minutes, then add in the carrot and celery you set aside. Continue to sauté until the carrots are soft, which will be approximately another 5 minutes.

Stir 1 tablespoon tomato paste or ketchup (whichever you have on hand) into the pan and add the entire mixture into the soup pot.

Toss in bay leaves, 1/2 teaspoon black pepper, dill and more salt to taste (approximately ½ tablespoon.)

Simmer for another 2 minutes or until your potatoes are fully cooked. (Consider them fully cooked when you can easily pierce them with a fork.)

. . .

"With this recipe," Daria said to June, "Some people like to add a spoonful of sour cream. Personally, I've tried both ways and I prefer the lighter taste without the sour cream."

RUSSIAN HONEY CAKE

Medovik Torte

When June arrived for her cooking lesson, Daria said, "I know you got a taste of this cake at Phil and Marg's wedding and wanted to learn how to make it. First, there are some interesting facts you should know."

"Oh yes," June replied. "Marvin has been drooling about that cake ever since he had a taste."

"This cake consists of eight paper-thin layers with sour cream spread on them—hence the other name it goes by, Sour Cream Cake, or Smetana Cake. It tastes like dreamy graham cracker that has been frosted."

"Mmm," June sighed.

"Most important," Daria said, "you must plan for two days to make this cake."

"Two days! I had no idea."

"Yes, you'll need to plan two hours on the first day and thirty minutes on the second day to finish it."

INGREDIENTS

Cake Layers
    1/2 cup (170 grams) honey
    1/2 cup (100 grams) sugar
    1/2 cup (115 grams) unsalted butter
    1 teaspoon baking soda
    3 large eggs
    1/4 teaspoon fine sea or table salt
    1 teaspoon (5 ml) vanilla extract
    3 1/2 cups (455 grams) all-purpose flour, divided

Frosting and Filling
    32 ounces sour cream (just shy of 4 cups or 900 grams)
    One 14-ounce can sweetened condensed milk (400 grams)

PREPARATION

Heat the oven to 350 degrees F. Then get two baking sheets (or round pizza pans), more if you have them. You will also need six sheets of parchment paper large enough to make a 9-inch circle.

"Now we are ready to begin," Daria said.

To make the cake dough
Take out a medium saucepan and combine the sugar, honey, and butter over medium heat. After it starts simmering, cook for another 3 to 4 minutes (at no exact temperature). You should notice it is becoming a bit darker and smells delightful. Beat in baking soda with a whisk. Remove from the stove and

set aside for a few minutes. You will not notice that it cools a lot, but it will settle a bit.

Use a spouted measuring cup or a small bowl to lightly beat your eggs.

Get the saucepan and begin whisking the honey mixture energetically into the pot while drizzling the thinnest stream (1/2 teaspoon at a time) of the eggs into the honey mixture. Do not stop mixing, but continue until all the eggs are thoroughly whisked in.

Stir in the salt and vanilla and 3 cups of the flour using a spoon. The dough will become thick like a bread. Stir in the remainder of the flour (1/2 cup), 1/4 cup at a time.

Lightly flour your work surface. Roll out the still-warm dough into one long piece and divide into 8 even pieces.

"I have another couple of tips here," Daria said as June wiped flour off her nose. "Sometimes the dough is a bit stiff. But just use a bit of pressure and you should be able to get your 8 pieces. Also, it works best to cut it when it is warm. If you find it is cooling down too quickly, put it into the microwave for 5 to 7 seconds to get it a bit warmer. A word of caution—you don't want to leave it too long and suddenly realize it is baking your dough."

Roll the first piece of dough between two pieces of parchment paper. The parchment does not need to be floured. Roll it slightly bigger than a 9-inch round.

Remove the top sheet of paper. Very lightly dust the top of the layer with flour before using the bottom of a 9-inch cake pan (or the rim of a 9-inch bowl) to trim the shape to an even circle.

Save any trimmings and put them aside on one of the

sheets of parchment paper. Do not worry if they overlap a little.

Poke the 9" circle all over with a fork. Then slide it onto a baking sheet and bake for 6 to 7 minutes; it should feel firm-ish and get slightly darker at the edges.

Tip: The parchment paper can now be used for another layer.

While the first layer is baking, roll out your second piece so it's ready to be popped into the oven as soon as the other one comes out. If possible, keep doing this and get the third ready. Continue to bake them two at a time. And continue to repeat this process until you have all eight baked.

June said, "Daria, I think I might need my timer while doing this, otherwise I might get too busy and burn them. I'm not sure how good a multi-tasker I am."

"I agree, that is a good idea," Daria said. "Another useful tip comes at the end. Take the sheet of parchment with all the cookie scraps, slide them onto a baking sheet and bake. Because these are the thinnest scraps, check them at 4 minutes because they will heat quickly. Remove from the oven at 5 minutes. They will now be a pale golden. Let them cool completely and save them to use to decorate, tomorrow."

Each time, after removing a layer from the oven, slide it onto a cooling rack to wait until you start frosting them.

Fill and frost the cake

With a clean whisk, whip the sour cream and sweetened condensed milk together in a large bowl.

Once the layers are cool, place a bit of the sour cream mixture on a plate and place the first layer on top of it.

"Center the layer on the plate," Daria advised. "I learned this the hard way. It will help adhere it in place."

Tear one of your used pieces of parchment paper into strips and use them to tuck all around the underside of the cake to protect the plate.

"It may seem like a very simple step, but trust me, if you don't do it, you will be sorry," Daria said.

Spoon 3/4 cup of the sour cream mixture onto the center of the first layer. Spread, leaving a good 1- to 2-inch margin of unfrosted layer.

"I like to sprinkle crushed layers of walnuts on each layer," Daria said. "I also have another tip—the sour cream is going to spill out and down the sides, creating a huge mess. It's also going to start sliding around and not remain neatly stacked. Before long, you will become aware that as the filling thickens, it will absorb into the cake layers."

Repeat until you have 8 layers stacked on top of each other. You can now put the cake in the fridge for one to three hours. At the end of that time, remove it from the fridge, and gently nudge the layers back into place if they have shifted.

Using a spoon and spatula, smooth the filling that has spilled onto the sides and top of the cake.

"Now this is my last tip for today," Daria said. "Don't worry about how it looks. We are going to let it chill overnight."

"Oh, Daria, this is going to be a masterpiece. You have given me so many great tips," June said before she left.

The next day, June and Daria got together to finish the cake.

Put the baked, reserved cookie scraps in a bag and roll them into crumbs with a rolling pin.

Take your cake out of the fridge and do a final clean-up of the frosting with a spatula. This includes spreading any pools of sour cream that are sitting on the cake plate up across the top and along the sides.

"This is one of my favorite steps," Daria said. "You can make a decoration on top of your cake. Take a piece of parchment and cut a stencil out of it. Then place it gently on top of your cake. Use a small spoon to sprinkle or gently spread the top and sides of the cake with the crumbs. Don't tell Tony, but sometimes I've used one of his small paintbrushes. Of course, I always check to see that they are clean. Then I gently brush the crumbs off the stencil and across the cake in a thin layer."

Remove the stencil and parchment paper strips and the cake is ready to serve. It can be served right away, or kept in the fridge for up to 5 days.

"Now, this is my final tip," Daria said. "It's hard to cut through eight layers, but I found that if I dip a knife in hot water, then I can make perfect cuts."

"Oh, Daria, thank you for walking me through this and

giving me so many great tips," June said when everything was all finished. "Marvin is going to be thrilled."

GLOSSARY

As each of the committee members came in and sat down, Bob began going around the table to take orders. "It's good to see everyone again," he greeted them.

Over and over again he heard, "It sure is good to be back."

Words like *tarasun, mors, kvas*, or *meduvokha* and orders of *draniki* seemed to go swirling around Shelley's head. Seeing the expression on her face, Gaspar said, "Don't worry, my *moi medvezhono*, you will be fine."

"Maybe we can go around the table and each give a word and its definition," Jenny suggested. "I'll begin."

———

Beef Stroganoff: Begin with a nice piece of beef, like a steak and cut it into little strips and mix it in *smetana* (sour cream).

Blini: A Russian pancake. To give you a few more details, *blini* is sometimes called *blin*. Traditionally it is made from wheat or buckwheat flour. For toppings it is suggested that it be served with sour cream, quark, butter, and other garnishes you may have in your fridge. They are also known as bliny, blintzes, crepes, or palatschinke.

Borscht: A sour cream soup made from beetroots. The main ingredient gives it a distinctive red colour.

Chicken Kiev: A dish made of a chicken fillet pounded and rolled in cold butter. Then it is rolled in a mixture of eggs and bread crumbs, and either fried or baked. It is traditionally served with rice or shoestring potatoes, both of which help to soak up the delicious herb butter filling. The meal is often completed with fresh string beans, peas, and broccoli.

Draniki: A very popular dish, these are Russian-style potato pancakes. The potatoes can be mashed, fried, baked, boiled, and then served with sour cream or apple sauce. Regardless of how you prepare it, it is very likely to become one of your top comfort foods. *Draniki* is very versatile. Some like it in the morning with eggs, whereas others prefer it with a salad at lunch. It is a wonderful side dish to any entrée.

Golubtsy: Cooked cabbage leaves wrapped around a variety of fillings. They are then baked, simmered, or steamed. Golubtsy is generally served with a sauce, such as tomato or sour cream.

Guriev kasha: This porridge is made from semolina and milk, with the addition of nuts, milk skins, and dried fruits. It was invented early in the 19th century by the chef Zakhar Kuzmin. Its name comes from the name of Count Dmitry Guriev, the Minister of Finance and a member of the State Council of the Russian Empire who, upon first tasting a dish of it, bought the chef, Zakhar Kuzmin, from his former employer. After that he ventured to promote the distribution of the recipe. Guriev kasha was also appreciated by Emperor Alexander III.

Russian Honey Cake: This cake consists of eight paper-thin cake layers with sour cream spread on them – hence the other name it goes by, Sour Cream Cake or Smetana Cake. It tastes like dreamy graham cracker which has been frosted.

Kvas: A fermented non-alcoholic beverage made from black or regular rye bread or dough.

Kissel: A fruit dessert of sweetened juice, thickened with arrowroot, cornstarch or potato starch.

Knish: A small savory pie filled with meat, potatoes, kasha, sauerkraut, onions, or cheese. It is baked or fried.

Medovik Torte: Russian honey cake. The honey is baked into the eight cake layers, which pairs perfectly with the alternate layers of sour cream frosting.

Medovukha: A traditional Russian honey-based drink.

Mimosa salad: It is often served as a tuna salad, although salmon or other fish can be used. It is layered with combinations hard-boiled eggs, potatoes, and carrots. Mimosa is often served as a lunch salad.

Mors: A non-carbonated Russian fruit drink prepared from berries. It can be made from many varieties of berries but commonly from lingonberry and cranberries. Sometimes blueberries, strawberries, or raspberries are used.

Oladi (Kefir) pancakes: Oladi are another version of pancakes. They are usually smaller in size. They are fried in oil, which gives them a lovely crunchy edge. They are best served hot with jam or sour cream.

Olivier Salad: A Russian version of potato salad. So of course, we start with diced potatoes, eggs, chicken or bologna, sweet peas and pickles with a mayonnaise dressing. Other vegetables, such as carrot or fresh cucumbers, can be added.

Pelmeni: A dumpling filled with a juicy meat centre. Many Russians considered it a classic comfort food.

Pirogi (pirozhki): Are made of a flaky or puff pastry.

They are often used as a dessert. They may be sweet and contain quark or cottage cheese. This base is then filled with fruits such as apples, plums, or berries. Other varieties have honey, nuts or poppy seeds. A savoury version is filled with meat, fish, mushrooms, cabbage, rice, buckwheat groats, or potato. These tasty little morsels are often served as an accompaniment to clear borscht, broth, or consommé.

Rassolnik: A classic soup made with barley, beef, potatoes, carrots, and... pickles. You mean cucumbers, right? Nope, pickles.

Sbiten: Since the 12th century, sbiten has been consumed as a traditional wintertime honey-based beverage. The key to excellent sbiten is good-quality honey and spices.

Sharlotka: Russian Sharlotka, interestingly enough, was actually invented in London in the 19th century by a French cook, Marie Antoine Careme. The Russian part came when it was served to Tsar Alexander I. In the beginning the name of the dish was *Charlotte à la Parisienne* (Parisian Sharlotka). Later on, the dessert was renamed Charlotte Russe and became famous all over the world.

Stewler: A fermented milk product, made by adding *smetana* (sour cream) to baked milk. It is very popular drink in Russia.

Tarasun: A highly alcoholic colourless liquid prepared by distillation and fermentation of mare's milk. It is described as a form of "milk whisky."

Zakuski: A variety of hors d'oeuvres, snacks, and appetizers, usually served buffet style. It often includes cold cuts, cured fish, mixed salads, *kholodets* (aspic), various pickled vegetables and mushrooms, *pirozhki*, caviar, deviled eggs, open sandwiches, canapés, and breads.

———

After all the foods were explained, Shelley sat back in her chair with her glass of *sbiten* and declared how overwhelmed she felt.

"Finish your drink and I'll walk you home," Gaspar said, offering her a brilliant smile.

"*Straight* home," Anna and Jenny called as they were leaving, only to be answered by Gaspar's smirk as he followed Shelley out.

As Gaspar and Shelley walked home, Shelley asked Gaspar, "What did you call me?"

"Oh, my *moi medvezhono*, which means my teddy bear. I was so proud of you, tonight."

"Hmm, I'm not sure how many words I will remember, but I have my trusty notes. Mostly I can't believe how much I've eaten since I've been here. No wonder my jeans are getting tight."

Gaspar went on, "I'm sure you've heard other words since you've been here. Do you want to take a guess as to their meaning?"

"Okay. This will be fun. Game on," Shelley responded. "**Babushka** is grandmother; whereas **Dedushka** is grandfather. **Mama** is mother; and **Papa** means father. **roditeli** means a parent; **roditeli** means several parents."

"Do you remember the greetings you learned at New Year's?"

"Well, I can't pronounce them, if that's what you mean."

"If I say, **Xristo's Voskress**—Christ has risen—you would say…"

"**Voistenno Voskress**—Christ is here. Right?"

"Right." As he drew her into a kiss, he said, "I will help you with the last few as they will require a few more details. **Ded Moroz** is the Russian equivalent of Santa Claus. He is really a winter wizard and wears a red and white heel-length furry coat. He's got a semi-round fur hat, and felt boots called *valenki* are on his feet. He also has a long white beard. In one hand he carries a staff which is considered magic, and he rides on a sleigh which is pulled by three horses abreast, known as a *troika*."

"Good so far," Shelley said.

"His granddaughter and helper, who accompanies him, is called Snegurochka, which translates to Snow Maiden. She wears a blue and white jacket and skirt. Her costume is completed with a snowflake crown and tall white boots, and she is noted for her rosy pink cheeks." Gaspar kissed her again. "Like yours."

―――――

AT PHIL AND MARG'S WEDDING

Common cup: toasting to a better life.

Tamada: Master of Ceremonies

Za-Molodykh: Toast for the newlyweds: "Cheers to the young couple that is presently getting married…"

Gor'ko: A protest that the wine is bitter, and the guests are wanting the couple to kiss for a long time to take out the bitter taste of the champagne (or vodka).

Marg's reference to a broken piece of china: The couple might stomp on a plate when they first enter their new home. The tradition is that whoever breaks the plate first will have the upper hand in the marriage. But they also have to bear in mind that the number of broken pieces equals the troubles they will face (which usually controls the stomping a bit!), and instead of catching the bouquet, anyone wishing to marry soon would place a piece of the plate under their pillow.

AFTERWORD

This book was written by three residents of Carewest Garrison Green long-term care facility, in Calgary, Alberta, Canada.

We have again enjoyed the experience of working together on this sequel to *Lighthouse in the Mist*. From a writing perspective we hope we have grown—it has certainly been a challenge to bring in bits and pieces from *Lighthouse in the Mist* and add teasers for the third book we wish to publish next year, *Changes in the Mist*.

We've enjoyed our evenings writing *Deep in the Mist* and we hope you have had just as much pleasure reading it.

You might leave a review on your favorite retailer's site to tell others about the books. And you can find both digital and print editions of the series online on the Amazon® store or in digital on the Kobo® store.

Lighthouse in the Mist
Deep in the Mist
Changes in the Mist

Made in the USA
Monee, IL
27 April 2021